He joined her at t
isn't everything."

Trying not to notice ho
felt, Allison turned to face him, her hip bumping up against his. "You didn't think that way eight years ago."

Cade tossed her a fond look and retorted gruffly, "Eight years ago I was a fool. No more."

He cradled her against his chest. His kiss was everything she desired, lush and evocative, searching, tempting. Her knees went weak, and her lips opened to the dizzying pressure of his—making out with him felt like the most intimate thing they could ever do.

Aware she was very close to falling for him all over again, Allison put her hand on his chest. Calling on every ounce of self-control she had, she broke off the kiss and stepped back, her emotions in turmoil.

"I don't know what I'm going to do with you," she murmured in exasperation, as her heart continued to race. He hadn't pursued her this avidly when they were actually dating!

"I don't know," he whispered playfully in return, rubbing his lips across the back of her knuckles. Once again, he searched her eyes. "Maybe kiss me back? Or better yet," he queried even more softly and tenderly, "give me a second chance?"

Dear Reader,

It can be hard to tell yourself the plain unvarnished truth. Especially when it comes to matters that are close to your heart. This is the situation Cade Lockhart and Allison Meadows find themselves in.

Cade knows he made the biggest mistake of his life choosing fame over love. Now that his professional baseball career is over, he wants to make amends. Pick up where he and Allison left off. The only problem is Allison can't even see them being casual friends, never mind in a relationship again.

Allison focused on her career after Cade broke her heart. Eight years later, she is on the brink of a success that is bigger than anything she ever imagined. If she achieves it, she will not have any room in her life for anything else, including the one man—the only man—she has ever loved. And while she tells herself work is enough, she has to wonder—is it?

Enter four Christmas matchmakers. The Bailey quadruplets love the holiday season! They think Allison and Cade should be together. The four-year-olds do everything they can to bring a renewed romance about. Because what's Christmas without a little mistletoe?

I hope you enjoy the second book of the Lockharts Lost & Found miniseries.

Happy reading and merry holidays!

Cathy Gillen Thacker

Four Christmas Matchmakers

CATHY GILLEN THACKER

HARLEQUIN

SPECIAL
EDITION

HARLEQUIN®
SPECIAL EDITION™

Recycling programs for this product may not exist in your area.

ISBN-13: 978-1-335-89486-1

Four Christmas Matchmakers

Harlequin Enterprises ULC
22 Adelaide St. West, 40th Floor
Toronto, Ontario M5H 4E3, Canada
www.Harlequin.com

Printed in U.S.A.

Cathy Gillen Thacker is a married mother of three. She and her husband reside in North Carolina. Her stories have made numerous appearances on bestseller lists, but her best reward is knowing one of her books made someone's day a little brighter. A popular Harlequin author, she loves telling passionate stories with happy endings and thinks nothing beats a good romance and a hot cup of tea! Visit her at cathygillenthacker.com for information on her books, recipes and a list of her favorite things.

Books by Cathy Gillen Thacker

Harlequin Special Edition

Lockharts Lost & Found

His Plan for the Quadruplets

Texas Legends: The McCabes

The Texas Cowboy's Quadruplets
His Baby Bargain
Their Inherited Triplets

Harlequin Western Romance

Texas Legends: The McCabes

The Texas Cowboy's Triplets
The Texas Cowboy's Baby Rescue

Visit the Author Profile page
at Harlequin.com for more titles.

Chapter One

"Gorgeous…"

Allison Meadows stepped away from the festive evergreen garland and home-crafted wreath she'd just placed on the front door of her Laramie, Texas, cottage. Both perfectly accentuated the gabled portico roof, her pale rose brick porch floor, stately white columns and sage-green door. She shook her head and let out a low, satisfied sigh. There was nothing as fun as decorating for Christmas!

"Are you talking to me or admiring your handiwork?"

Allison hadn't heard her "guest" approach, but she did not have to turn around to know whom that low, sexy voice belonged to—Cade Lockhart. Inveterate charmer. And onetime love of her life…turned giant pain in the tuchus. Mostly because he likely kept telling himself that after everything that had happened between them, they could still be friends.

Glad she had finished her latest blog post, she switched off the video camera that had been recording her work. Turned around. And squared off with the former star pitcher for the Texas Wranglers pro baseball team.

She was well used to his six-foot-three frame. Tall men in Texas were a dime a dozen. The short mussed sable-brown hair, mesmerizing espresso eyes and intractable jaw were a little harder to disregard. As were his sensual lips. After all, she knew how he kissed. Touched. And did a whole host of other things. Hence, as their gazes locked, she felt her heart take a telltale leap. Although she couldn't help reminding herself there was no reason a wicked sense of humor, warm seductive smile and solid male muscle should be such a turn-on.

"Who or what was I talking about?" she echoed, picking up the threads of the conversation. Though, technically speaking, he was right. *Gorgeous* fit. She lifted her chin. "What do you think?"

He grinned at her deadpan tone. "A little of both."

Refusing to be drawn in by the inherent mischief in his gaze, she smiled sweetly. Not about to admit she'd always thought he was incredibly gorgeous, too. "Then you'd be wrong," she corrected archly.

His gaze drifted over her face, lingered on her lips, before returning to her eyes. "I don't think so."

This was not an argument she was going to win.

Her heart racing, Allison gathered the hammer and nails she'd left on the rail and put them back into the toolbox at her feet. She snapped the lid shut, then turned back to face him. "I thought we agreed we were going to do everything we could to avoid running into each other now that we are both living back in Laramie…" Although she didn't expect him to stay in his hometown for long. Just until his unpopularity in Dallas completely died down. And people forgot about the disappointing end to the Texas Wranglers' season.

He scrubbed a hand underneath his handsome jaw. "Actually, as I recall, that was your dictum, not mine."

"Necessary, in any case."

"Not in my opinion," he said flatly.

And here they went again…

He stepped closer, persisting, "All I did was try to send some interior design business your way when you were first starting out."

Allison swallowed around the parched feeling in her throat. "By having me decorate the house you were buying back in Dallas without letting me know the owner was you?"

He straightened, squaring his broad shoulders. "I had my reasons for doing that."

"Can't wait to hear them."

He squinted, displeased. "Okay, well, *first*, I figured you'd reject my request if I asked."

Sharing in his obvious exasperation, Allison glared right back at him. "You would have been right about that," she said stonily, then pulled her cell phone from her pocket to see if the work email she'd been expecting had come in yet. To her disappointment, it hadn't. "I would have turned you down flat."

Victorious to have been proved right about that much, he braced his hands on his waist and continued, "*Second*, I was warned by my business manager that the subcontractor charges would likely be a whole lot higher if it were known that the property being renovated would soon belong to the rookie pitcher for the Texas Wranglers. Because it would be assumed, as beneficiary of a new multimillion-dollar contract, that I would not know how to handle my money. And would go around spending like a drunken sailor."

She took in his nondescript charcoal-gray running clothes and expensive sneakers. "So to prove otherwise, you hired a rookie designer who also happened to be dirt cheap by celebrity standards."

His broad shoulders flexed. "Is that what your ire

is about?" He speared her with his gaze. "You think I didn't pay you enough for your work?"

"No." He had paid her plenty through his accountant. More than she had hoped to get. Which, for reasons she couldn't quite fathom, still rankled even more.

"Then...?" he prodded, wanting the rest of her explanation.

Trying not to recall how taut and warm his muscled body felt after a run, she ignored everything else he had done to hurt her, albeit unintentionally, in his unrelenting drive for success. Admitting in abject embarrassment, "I thought I was doing a house for the bachelor CEO of CBL Enterprises."

"And you were," he explained patiently, pacing back and forth on her wide front porch, "because that was me." He paused, his back to a pillar.

Her temper flaring, Allison remained beneath the high gabled roof and sputtered angrily, "Except I didn't *know* it was you until a reporter from the style section of the Dallas newspaper asked me how I landed the gig and if it had anything to do with the fact we had dated all through high school and college."

Then, she recalled in consternation, the female journalist had gone on to imply a romantic reconciliation just *might* be in the works.

When she had known, deep in her gut, that such an occurrence would never happen. Not after the way he had neglected her at the end of their relationship.

Well used to such invasions of privacy, Cade pushed away from the pillar and offered a maddeningly affable shrug. "You could have just declined to answer. Or pushed the conversation to something a lot more interesting."

"And made matters worse?" Allison scoffed.

He scowled in exasperation. "I don't know what you're complaining about. The gig got you a write-up in the paper and a lot of attention."

And a lot of work, she thought. Initially, mostly from baseball fans who wanted to ask her about Cade and what he was really like. But that was not the point. She stepped closer to him. "I was humiliated and embarrassed to be caught unaware."

He towered over her. "And I told you at the time I was sorry about that." He reminded her of the multiple phone messages he had left—all of which had gone unanswered. His voice turned unexpectedly penitent. "It was never my intention to make you feel foolish."

At the time, Allison had been too hurt and angry to respond to anything he'd had to convey. She had simply wanted them to never speak again. But now that eight years had passed, she had to know.

"Then what was your intention?" she asked.

Easy, Cade thought. *To share in my good fortune. And begin to make up for the way I treated you the entire last year or so we were together.* The birthdays and anniversaries he'd forgotten. The dates he'd canceled so he could get in a little more practice. The calls and texts he'd made that had been so brief and hurried they'd practically been nonexistent. She'd been a saint, whereas he'd been the world's worst boyfriend. It was no surprise she had finally seen the light and broken up with him. No surprise he'd regretted it ever since.

Not that she was interested in letting him find a way back to her.

Trying to figure out how much—if anything—to say about all that, he let his gaze roam over her. Her five-foot-seven-inch height and slender frame always left him wanting to step in to protect her. As usual these days, she was more dressed up than was warranted for a weekday afternoon. Her plaid knee-length kilt a bit retro. But sexy nonetheless. Black tights encased her showgirl-worthy legs. A dark green turtleneck sweater cloaked her luscious breasts and brought out the vibrant hue of her long-lashed eyes. But it was her pretty face, pert nose, stubborn chin and kissably soft lips that most haunted his dreams.

Dreams that had only gotten hotter and more fre-quent the last three months.

"I was trying to help you," he said.

Indignant color flooded her high-sculpted cheeks. "I didn't need your help." As always, when in a tem-per, she tossed her shoulder-length dark brown hair.

He lifted both hands in abject surrender. "I know that now."

She clamped her lips together tightly. Appearing as if it were taking every ounce of self-control she had not to haul off and slug him. "Good."

Man. She was still really ticked off at him. That meant she still had to harbor some feelings for him, right? He held her eyes for a long moment, giving her all the respect she was due. "Your blog is incredibly successful," he said admiringly. "And getting more so every day. All the women I know read it."

Still glaring at him furiously, she huffed. "But not you."

The truth was, he never missed a post. But figuring she would think he was insincerely kissing up to her if he admitted to being her biggest cheerleader, he merely shrugged.

"*The Cottage Site* isn't really my thing," he fibbed, deliberately getting the name wrong—just to get under her skin and keep her there talking to him a little while longer.

His facetious mistake had the desired effect. She pushed the words through tightly gritted teeth. "The name is *My Cottage Life.*"

They were standing on the porch of said cottage. Talking, well…arguing…more than they had in years.

"So, if that's all…" she said dismissively.

Cade sobered. They really had gotten sidetracked. "Actually, it's not."

* * *

Of course it wasn't all, Allison thought. Cade was an expert at delaying her. Keeping the attention on himself. Especially now that he was out of the limelight.

"I wanted to talk to you about this weekend," he continued, even more seriously.

She held up a hand, ready to decline whatever he had in mind. "I'm babysitting for the Bailey quadruplets while their parents are in Switzerland."

"I know. Shawn mentioned it." Intuitive dark brown eyes lassoed hers. "He said you are refusing to bring in extra help and he's concerned."

Allison turned her gaze to the wintry gray clouds looming on the horizon. It wasn't supposed to storm this evening, but it still looked like it might. "I've already talked to Sarabeth about the situation. She isn't concerned."

Cade inched closer, inundating her with his soap and man scent. "The thing is, I offered to help out, too."

She could barely look at him and not wonder what it would be like to kiss him again. Just as an experiment, of course. To find out if her outrageously hot memories of the two of them were wildly exaggerated, too?

Allison rubbed at the tension gathering in her temples and drew a long, bolstering breath. Regarding him from beneath her lashes, she asked, "Since when do you babysit four-year-olds? Never mind four at once!"

"Since I heard you planned to go it alone."

Wishing she didn't enjoy spending time with him quite so much, even under these ridiculously aggravating circumstances, she picked up her toolbox, looked him in the eye and flashed him a confident smile. There was *no way* she was going to amuse him while he was temporarily at loose ends, trying to figure out his next move, only to have him break her heart all over again. Once had been enough!

"Well, un-volunteer," she snapped.

She watched his cocky grin disappear.

Tamping down the fast beat of her heart, she went on in a low, quelling tone. "I mean it, Cade. I do not need or want your help with babysitting the quadruplets or anything else!" Leaving him alone to contemplate *that*, she walked inside the house, shutting the door behind her.

Chapter Two

"Thanks for doing this for us," Shawn Bailey told Cade the following morning, carrying two suitcases down to their car.

His wife, Sarabeth, stood nearby, their aging black Labrador retriever on a leash at her side. "Zeus is really too old to be boarded these days."

Aware how quiet it was with the girls already at school for the day, Cade smiled. "Hey, I'm happy to help." He paused to pet the white-faced dog, whose tail wagged arthritically, then went to get the dog food and dishes that they'd packed up for him. After carrying Zeus's belongings to his pickup truck, and setting them in the back, he returned to the porch for the dog bed. That, too, went in the back seat of his four-door Silverado. "I haven't had a dog in a long time. It will be nice to have one around again."

"The quadruplets are going to miss Zeus," Sarabeth predicted, still holding on to the leash. "They've never really been away from him."

Or their mom, either, Cade thought. Since it was Shawn who traveled constantly for his job as tech company sales VP, and Sarabeth who stayed in Laramie with the kids. A fact that seemed to have taken a toll on their marriage, if the aloofness between them was any indication.

Predictably, Shawn dismissed the worry. "They'll be fine," he said. "Although speaking of our girls." He looked at Cade. "I understand you won't be helping out Allison after all."

"She wasn't too happy we even suggested it." Sarabeth sighed, moving even closer to their dog, petting the very top of Zeus's head. "Which makes me wonder if I should even go."

Cade knew that would be a mistake, if the couple wanted to get their relationship on a better footing. "Hey, you have to be there for Shawn's big award. Luxury hotel. Champagne and room service. Prime skiing. You have to go."

Shawn looked at his wife, with just a fraction of the hope he'd possessed when they had married seven years prior. Sarabeth tensed, her reluctance coming through loud and clear.

"I'll make sure everything is fine here," Cade re-assured her.

Sarabeth hesitated. "But if Allison won't let you help…"

He was still hoping he could change that deci-sion. "Then I'll enlist my family or some of the other moms from the Laramie Multiples Club. She's a lot less likely to say no to any of them."

Sarabeth tensed. "I just hate to impose, especially during the holidays because everyone is so busy."

Shawn looked at his watch. Done arguing. "We really need to leave, honey. It's going to take us two and a half hours to get to the Dallas airport."

Cade walked with them to his pal's car. "Allison will be fine," he predicted. "You know what a perfec-tionist she is. She probably has everything planned down to the last second." In fact, she'd still be orga-nizing every second of *their* life if they had stayed together.

"I know." Sarabeth sighed again. She turned the leash over to Cade. "That's kind of what worries me…"

Figuring if he stayed much longer Sarabeth really would talk herself out of going, Cade wished them a good weekend, then headed down the sidewalk and helped Zeus into the front seat of his pickup truck. The Lab sighed loudly and lay down across the bench seat, then put his head in Cade's lap.

"I hate to do this to you," he said, "but I'm going

to have to run off almost as soon as I get you settled at my place. I have an appointment this morning. And it's one that really has to go well," he added, as Zeus looked up at him, listening intently. "I promise, though, I'll take good care of you."

The pooch snuggled closer.

Back at his place, Cade took everything inside. Set up Zeus's bed and water dish, then went to change clothes. By the time he returned, the Lab was already curled up in his bed, his chin resting on the bolster edge. Cade knelt to pet him. "See you later, buddy."

Zeus looked up at him, as if silently trying to communicate something. What, Cade wasn't sure. Wondering if he were already homesick, Cade reassured him, "Your family is going to be fine."

Zeus's brow furrowed.

"Sarabeth and Shawn will be back from their trip before you know it."

Zeus continued to stare.

Cade scratched him behind the ear. "The quadruplets will be with Allison. I know you'd like to be there, too, but she's been pretty clear. She doesn't need any assistance."

Zeus made a short snorting sound of disagreement.

Cade rolled his eyes, sharing the Labrador's frustration. "Yeah, well, that's my ex for ya. I can't exactly change her, not at this late date."

Zeus lifted one eyebrow, then the other. His eyes

remained locked on Cade's, beseeching silently. "I promise," he said firmly, giving him a final pat. "If there's trouble, we'll find a way to help. Whether Allison wants us to or not."

In the meantime, he had a very important meeting to attend.

To Allison's relief, retrieving the girls from preschool went smoothly. Of course, all she had to do was drive Sarabeth's Suburban through the pickup line and wait while the prekindergarten volunteer moms shepherded Amber, Jade, Sienna and Hazel to the SUV and loaded them inside the vehicle. As soon as all the safety harnesses were on, she followed the directions of the dad directing traffic and eased away from the school, heading back to the Bailey home.

And it was only when they walked inside that trouble started. Amber looked around and saw Zeus's downstairs dog bed was missing. "Where's Zeus?" she demanded in concern. Like her three sisters, she had chin-length naturally curly brown hair and cornflower blue eyes. They were allowed to pick out their own clothes, so they only dressed alike on special occasions. Today, in deference to the chilly winter weather, they were wearing wool socks and sneakers, corduroy pants and turtleneck tops in a rainbow of colors.

Determined to get off to an organized start, Allison helped the girls off with their coats and hung them up in the front hall closet, while they took their backpacks and empty reusable lunch sacks to the kitchen. "Zeus is staying with Cade Lockhart while your mom and dad are away, remember?"

"But I want him here!" Sienna said stubbornly.

Jade moved closer to Allison and curled her fingers in Allison's wool skirt. "He might be lonely."

Hazel did a series of cartwheels through the front hall alongside the staircase, then stuck her index fingers at the edges of her mouth, wrinkled her nose and pulled her lips taut while making a goofy face. "I want to go get him!" she said.

"Me, too!" Amber chimed in.

"I'll get his leash," Jade said, eager to help. She frowned, staring at the newel post where it was usually looped. "It's gone, too!"

Amber started to cry loudly. Her sisters joined in. Soon, all four were sobbing as if their hearts would break. Allison did her best to calm them. To no avail. One minute passed, then several more, and they were still all completely distraught.

Not sure what to do, just knowing she couldn't possibly call Sarabeth for advice because their plane for Switzerland had already taken off from Dallas, she took her cell phone into the kitchen and, referring to the emergency numbers left on the front of the fridge, called Cade. To her relief, he picked up right away. "What's going on there?" he said.

Allison tried talking, but he couldn't hear her,

even when she shouted to be heard over the din. So she stepped into the laundry room and shut the door behind her. The racket could still be heard, but it was muted now. "The girls miss Zeus!"

"Want me to bring him over for a visit?" Cade asked.

Grateful to find him sounding helpful instead of smug, given how positive she had been that his assistance would not be necessary, she drew a bolstering breath. "Can you?"

Cade paused, and just like that, she could picture him trying to work out the logistics, his ruggedly handsome face creased with concern.

"Yeah. It's going to take me about twenty minutes to get there, because I'm not home right now, but I can do that."

In the living room, the sobbing increased exponentially. Abruptly, they weren't the only ones who needed a much stronger shoulder to lean on. "The sooner the better." Allison pushed the words around the growing lump in her throat.

"In the meantime," he said, as gentle as always in traumatic moments like this, "why don't you let me talk to them for a second."

Allison opened the laundry room door. "Okay. I'll try." She walked back into the living room, where the drama continued. While she had no doubt the girls were genuinely sad, and a little worried because this was the first time since they were born that they had been away from both parents for more than a few hours at a time, she could also see there was a little bit of the budding thespians in the situation. Because they were now definitely trying to outdo each other with operatic intensity.

She put Cade on speaker and signaled a time-out. "Girls!" she shouted. "Cade wants to talk to you about Zeus!"

To her surprise, they immediately stopped wailing.

"Girls." Cade's voice rumbled out of the cell phone speaker. "Zeus misses you, too, and I'm going to bring him right over, but it's going to take me a little while to get there. So, are you cool with that? Because if you-all keep crying like that, you're probably going to scare him," Cade warned dramatically. "Or at least make him *very* sad."

Amber smeared the moisture from her face. "We'll stop crying."

"We promise," Jade agreed.

Sienna looked only partly mollified but finally said, "Okay." While Hazel went back to making goofy faces and doing cartwheels around the room.

"You got this, Allie?" Cade asked.

It had been a long time since he had called her that. Too long.

"I do," Allison said. She switched off speaker, then, feeling a little more rattled than she cared to admit, murmured ever so softly, "Just don't take too long."

* * *

"Wow. It's really peaceful in here, considering what it sounded like twenty minutes ago." Cade strolled in, Zeus at his side. He was surprisingly dressed up in an expensive sport coat that brought out the espresso of his eyes, a button-up shirt that was a single shade lighter and coordinating tie. Instead of the tailored slacks she imagined went with the pricey ensemble, he was wearing dark denim jeans and boots.

Beginning to feel a little embarrassed to have been so quick to sound the alarm, she said, "The girls calmed down the instant they heard you were coming over. They went upstairs to play while they were waiting."

"No surprise there," he teased. "I have that effect on all the ladies."

Acutely aware she'd been relieved to have him rushing to their rescue, too, Allison rolled her eyes. "And humble, too."

He chuckled, the sound as soothing as it was arousing. His handsome face splitting into the wide, charming grin she'd never quite stopped dreaming about, Cade bent to unsnap the leash from the black Lab's collar.

Schooling herself to calm down, Allison called up the stairs, "Girls? Cade is here with Zeus!"

Excited squeals followed. All four girls came running, each of them looking disheveled in different ways. Amber had her sleeves rolled up past her elbows. Sienna's hair was falling out of her barrette. Hazel had taken her socks off and was barefoot. Jade had exchanged her corduroy pants for a pair of shorts.

"Zeus!" they yelled in unison. Amber knelt to hug his head. The others followed suit, draping themselves across his body and burying their faces in his sleek, shiny coat.

"We missed you so much!"

"Don't leave us again!"

"We need you, sweet puppy!"

Oh, dear, Allison thought, locking glances with Cade. How were the girls going to react when she had to tell them Zeus was leaving with Cade again? Not well, it appeared, since he seemed a little concerned, too.

Amber let go of Zeus's head and straightened up. "Is our after-school snack ready yet?" she asked.

"Not yet," Allison answered, aware Sarabeth usually scheduled that for 4:00 p.m. "But soon." She wanted to do things as normally as possible. Sticking to a schedule always helped.

"Then can we go upstairs and play some more while we wait?" Sienna asked happily.

"Sure," she said.

The girls darted off, running up the stairs. Figuring she owed him something for his trouble, Allison asked, "Would you like to stay for tea with us?"

Zeus made his way to the space where his bed usually sat beneath the front windows and lay down with a contented sigh.

Cade ambled closer and gave her a slow, thorough once-over. "Tea?"

Aware he had always been more of a straight black coffee guy, Allison led the way past the L-shaped sofa dominating the large open living space to the kitchen, where she'd been working both before and after she'd picked up the girls. The Carrara marble island top was covered with homemade goodies. Delicate tea cakes, picked up from the Sugar Buzz bakery in town and covered in holiday shades of white, green and red, were arranged on a crystal dish.

She'd already put together a platter of beautifully arranged tiny chicken salad sandwiches. "The girls will be having raspberry lemonade. I wanted them to have something special. But I was going to have tea." She pointed to the kettle on the stove. "I could fix you coffee or some other beverage, as well."

"Water is fine." He lifted a brow in the direction of her camera on the opposite counter and the video recorder on the tripod. Came toward her. "What's going on here?"

Her heartbeat picked up again for no reason she could figure. She cleared her throat. "I'm working on tomorrow's post."

"You're going to write about babysitting?"

Allison returned his assessing look. "No. Of course

not." She moved to put the island between them and went back to what she'd been doing before he'd rung the doorbell. "My blog is about living the happily single life of a professional woman. Preparing to host an afternoon tea, though, is something my readers really enjoy."

He watched her layer thin slices of cucumber on top of cream cheese, then put the crustless rectangles of bread together into dainty tea sandwiches, the same shape and size as the others.

His gaze drifted over her white cashmere sweater and green wool skirt. "Also explains why you're so dressed up."

Glad for the extra height her heels gave her, she said, "But not why you are."

For a moment, she thought he might tell her what he had been up to that required such fancy duds, but the moment passed and all he did was shrug.

He turned his glance to the second floor. "Awfully quiet up there."

Too quiet, he seemed to think.

After the riot of tears and drama earlier? "I don't see that as a bad thing," Allison murmured.

The grooves on either side of his mouth deepened. "You wouldn't. Given the fact you were an only child."

The sounds of several doors opening and closing came from upstairs. He remained where he was and continued listening intently, while Allison tried not to notice how handsome he was. An impossible task. Ignoring the tingle of sizzling awareness zipping through her, she retorted, "What's that supposed to mean?" She hated it when he implied she was clueless.

He continued standing there, hands on his hips. The edges of his sport coat brushed back to reveal his sinewy chest, trim waist and taut middle. With a crooked grin, he reminded her, "I grew up with four sisters and three brothers. And whenever *we* were that quiet, it was only because we were doing something we didn't want discovered."

More footsteps could be heard scampering across the floors overhead, signaling the girls were beginning to get a little more rambunctious.

Allison recalled his crew of siblings. They had definitely been rowdy in their younger days.

Shawn and Sarabeth's girls were different, however.

Yes, they had been overwrought earlier, but that was before Zeus had arrived to comfort them. "I'm sure they are fine," she reiterated firmly.

"Maybe one of us should check on them anyway," Cade said.

Allison was about to tell him that really wasn't necessary when her cell phone rang. She looked down at the screen, unable to help her mouth opening in a delighted "oh" of surprise.

"Who is it?" he asked.

"Laurel Grimes," Allison admitted joyfully. "An executive producer from the Home Interior Television Network!"

* * *

Cade watched Allison turn her back to him, lift the phone to her ear and say hello. "No. It's a perfect time," she murmured silkily.

Upstairs, he could hear the patter of little feet. Running in one direction, then another. More doors softly opening and closing.

And still Allison talked animatedly. "Absolutely! Yes, of course… I would love to meet Tripp Taylor. Oh, and I'd be happy to do the initial interview via Skype at his convenience, whenever that is. Thank you! Yes, see you soon."

She ended the call.

"I take it that was good news," Cade remarked, his gaze drifting over her.

Eyes sparkling happily, she moved close enough he could catch a whiff of her jasmine perfume. It was every bit as feminine and enticing as she was. "Very good news. Laurel said Tripp, the programming director of HITN, wants to meet me, too."

He trod carefully. "About…?"

Blushing, Allison placed her hands on the counter on either side of her. She drew in a deep, enervating breath that lifted the soft swell of her breasts. "I'm in the running for a new TV show aimed at thirty-something women who are contentedly single."

"Sounds like a perfect fit."

She turned toward the stove. Taking the kettle off,

she poured hot water into the ceramic teapot. Let it sit. "Well, I haven't gotten it yet."

Cade had always believed in her, the way she had believed in him. "You will." Given how pretty and accomplished and talented she was, they'd be crazy not to take her.

"I don't know about that." Allison emptied the newly warmed teapot. Then inserted several spoonfuls of loose tea, added more steaming water and put on the lid. Leaving it to steep, she turned back to him. "Jennifer Moore is the other lifestyle blogger still in the running."

Cade watched the silky ends of her dark hair brush the tops of her slender shoulders. It was shorter now, more sophisticated than when they'd been together. But just as touchable.

Pushing aside his desire to take her in his arms and offer his congratulations that way, Cade remained where he was. "Never heard of her."

"Well, you will." Allison compressed her soft lips. "Jennifer Moore is also a single woman in her thirties and she is a fabulous lifestyle influencer and blogger. She's an oil heiress and a lot more bachelorette and less do-it-yourself-ish than me, but her emphasis is also on living the best life you can. Her blog *City Lights* has the same core audience and has been growing every bit as fast as mine has."

Zeus came into the kitchen, moving faster than usual. He stared at both Allison and Cade, and when they weren't sure what he was trying to tell them, he nudged the back of Cade's knee with his nose. Once, and then again. Harder this time.

"What is it, buddy?" he asked gently.

Allison added, "Do you need to go outside?"

Zeus gave a little snort and swiveled his head around, as if directing Cade back in the direction they all had come. The Lab turned and began walking that way, stopped and looked back at them beseechingly, and walked again.

Perplexed, Cade and Allison both fell into step beside him. It was extremely quiet upstairs again. Nothing was amiss in the living area. Except for... Was that a small puddle of *liquid* on the foyer floor? Next to the staircase?

Zeus walked over to it, stood, staring down at it.

And that was when they both heard the plop, plop, plop of water falling. In tandem, they looked through the front windows. It wasn't raining outside. Then they turned in the direction Zeus was staring.

"Oh, no," Allison gasped, moving toward the staircase that led to the second floor. There, on the edge of the top tread, a river of water flowed.

Chapter Three

Allison raced up the staircase, Cade right behind her. As she reached the top, her shoe hit the saturated stair runner and then, in the hall, soggy wall-to-wall carpet.

Sienna was standing in front of the open linen closet doors, a wet baby doll clutched to her chest, a towel in hand. Jade was in her bedroom, busily taking every item of clothing out of her dresser drawers. Amber was soundlessly emptying her toy bin while Hazel came out of the hall bathroom—a sun hat placed jauntily on her head, a baby doll in her arms, rubber rain boots on her feet.

"What in the world is going on?" Allison cried.

Cade leaped to turn off the spigot on the overflowing bathtub as a six-inch-high wall of water escaped out the door into the upstairs hall.

"Towels!" he ordered, plunging his arm, sport coat and all, into the flooded tub to open up the drain.

He was of the right mindset, Allison thought. They could sort this all out later. "Girls, help me!" she ordered frantically.

She began tossing out stacks of towels, throwing some to Cade, others directly onto the bathroom floor and a bunch to the girls themselves. And still water gushed out into the upstairs hall, moving up to their ankles, where she stood.

"Mop up the water!" Cade instructed, while Zeus watched patiently from down below, as if sensing that if he were to come up, he would only be in the way.

Finally, the mini-lake of water had dissipated. Once the tub was fully drained, he grabbed the sopping wet towels one at a time and put all twenty or so into the basin.

"How's the hall carpet?" he asked Allison.

"Completely saturated." To the point she was beginning to wonder if the ceiling below would eventually collapse.

"We're going to need help." He pulled his phone from his pocket, quickly scrolled through. "I'm calling Laramie Restoration."

While he explained the situation, Allison headed

for the master bathroom. There were another six towels in there. She took them back into the hallway and laid them on the carpet, doing her best to soak up as much moisture as she could. Then she turned to the four girls.

After removing her own sopping wet shoes, she grabbed four fresh pairs of socks and pants, then ushered the quadruplets, and their baby dolls, downstairs. When everyone was dry again, and sitting in the kitchen, she asked, "What in the world were you all thinking?"

"We were just playing," Sienna declared stubbornly.

"Yeah," Jade explained, wiggling her toes. "We wanted to take our baby dolls swimming."

"Only we couldn't find our swimsuits, only theirs," Amber explained, petting Zeus, who had come over to cuddle with her.

"We were being quiet," Hazel said, seeming to think that quiet equaled good in this instance.

Allison buried her face in the palms of her hands.

Cade appeared in the doorway. Looking big and strong and masculine, he sauntered into the kitchen. "We're in luck. The restoration company has a crew that can be here in fifteen minutes to suction up any remaining water upstairs. Pull the carpet in the hall. And put out the fans and dehumidifier so everything will dry out."

Four sets of eyes turned to the repast Allison had been preparing. "I'm hungry," Amber declared.

"Me, too," Sienna agreed.

"Can we have some tea?" Jade asked.

"And drink it like this?" Hazel held out her pinkie and giggled.

Aware her babysitting gig had started out on an especially disastrous note, Allison nodded wearily and rose. Too late, she realized she should have listened to Cade's advice when he'd warned her something might be going on with the girls.

He hung his jacket over the back of a chair and rolled up his damp sleeves to just below the elbow. Then loosened his tie and undid the top button on his dress shirt. "I'm curious," he said, squinting down at their young charges. "Is this something you would have done if your parents were home?"

Guilty looks all around. "Well," Amber finally allowed, speaking for the group, "maybe if we were outside and Mommy said it was okay to get in our baby pool."

Hazel accused petulantly, "Allison just said to play nicely. She didn't say what."

"That's true," Allison said, burying her face in her hands yet again. And as hard as it was to admit, Cade was right. As an only child who hadn't babysat since she was a preteen, what did she know about taking care of pre-K quadruplets?

"Still," he chastised gently, "I'm guessing you all knew better."

Silence fell. Reluctant nods all around.

Allison got up to bring the platters of tea sandwiches and petits fours to the table, along with six plates and some napkins.

"So, don't you think you owe Allison an apology?" he asked.

More nods. Big sighs. "We're sorry," the girls chimed in unison.

Jade bit her lip. "Are you going to tell our mommy and daddy?"

Allison looked at Cade. Surprisingly, they were in agreement. "No," she said solemnly, pouring raspberry lemonade for the girls while Zeus settled in his spot underneath the table. "I'm not going to tell your parents. Not right now. As long as you don't do anything like this again."

The girls exchanged looks. Sober now. "We won't," they promised.

"What about Santa?" Hazel asked. "Are you going to tell him?"

Allison looked at Cade. Again, she found they were of the same sentiment. "No," she said.

The girls breathed a sigh of relief. "Good. Because we do not want to be on the Naughty list," Sienna declared fervently. Her sisters agreed.

Talk then turned to the general rules of the house when Mommy and Daddy were home. Allison and

Cade made sure the girls understood the same standards applied when Sarabeth and Shawn were not home.

By the time they had finished their tea, the three workers from the restoration company had arrived. Allison bundled up the girls and took them out to the backyard to play, and Cade stayed inside to lend a hand there while the water extraction machinery was utilized. He came to get them when all was clear.

Allison went upstairs with the girls to inspect the second-floor hallway. The fan and dehumidifier were going. The hall carpeting and padding had been removed, leaving only a wooden subfloor in place.

"Where are all the towels and the bath mats?" Allison asked.

"I carried it all down to the laundry room and started a load," Cade told her.

She met his gaze, not sure there would ever be words to explain how grateful she was for his calm in the midst of this crisis. Not to mention his lack of judgment or recriminations. "That was helpful," she praised him sincerely.

He favored her with a sexy half smile. "I aim to please."

Exactly what she'd feared. That this comradery would somehow lead to physical and emotional closeness, and she couldn't risk being that vulnerable to him again. Not when she'd made a life that was perfect without him in it. Or *nearly* perfect. "Girls, how about you go to your rooms and begin cleaning up your toys and putting them back in the toy chests? Then I'll come up to help you with your clothes."

As they dispersed to their rooms, Cade and Allison lingered in the upstairs hall. She looked around. "We're lucky Zeus alerted us and we caught it when we did. Otherwise the ceiling could have collapsed."

"But it didn't."

Her pulse raced at the gentle undertone in his low voice. It was hard to imagine how overwhelmed she would have been had he not been here to help. Or how much she enjoyed leaning on those broad shoulders of his again. "Are they going to be able to save the carpet?"

He walked the length of the hall, inspecting as he went. "Oh, yeah, they just need to dry it out first. The carpet pad underneath will have to be replaced, but that's not much." He returned to her side.

"How much is all this going to cost?"

He shrugged his brawny shoulders, as self-assured as ever. "I've got it covered."

She propped her hands on her hips, aware of the fact she was now barefoot, which gave him an eight-inch height advantage. "Cade…"

He cut her off with a lift of his big calloused palm. "It's already taken care of."

His willingness to take responsibility for something that clearly wasn't his fault, along with the reminder he had hit the big time while she was still struggling to make it, brought forth a wellspring of humiliation and resentment. "I can't let you do that."

Suddenly seeming a little embarrassed, he said gruffly, "Already done."

When she would have continued protesting, he explained, "The owner of the restoration company is a big Texas Wranglers fan. He knows I still have connections with the team, and he agreed to help us out in exchange for a set of tickets for opening night next spring for him and his entire crew. So, I made the call. And it's done."

"Oh." Of course, he'd been able to play the celebrity card. Why hadn't she realized that? And why was she allowing the fact that he was still more successful than her, professionally, bother her so? It wasn't as if he had edged away from her, back when they'd been dating, because she hadn't been good enough to be on the arm of a major leaguer…was it?

His voice turned husky with regret. "Besides, if I hadn't been distracting you, the tub might never have overflowed."

Allison wasn't positive of that. She had been pretty wrapped up in her own world. Preparing tea for her blog. Taking a work phone call…

"Allison…we need help…" One by one, the girls appeared in the doorway of their bedrooms, their expressions pitiful.

"I'll be right there," she promised. Taking his arm,

she guided him in the direction she wanted him to go. "First, I have to walk Cade out."

His bicep swelled beneath her fingers. "Sure you don't want me to stay and assist?" he asked.

She shook her head and continued escorting him down the stairs. It was far too tempting to lean on him as it was...the way she had when they were young...

Knowing Allison hadn't really thought this decision out, Cade persisted, "There's a lot of picking up to do. And I doubt the girls are going to get very far on their own. At least with the organizing of their dresser drawers."

Allison sashayed her way back to the laundry room. "You'd be surprised how adept I am at things like that."

He imagined he would be surprised about a lot of things.

She plucked his socks out of the dryer and handed them to him. "Besides, don't you have plans this evening with some of your arm candy?"

So she'd heard the talk that he'd had plenty of female visitors from Dallas during the last year, especially when it looked as if he would fully recover from his injury and go back to being the star pitcher he had been. And that he liked to go on group rather than individual dates, because the expectations on him for any kind of intimacy were a lot less.

He sat down to pull on his socks, then his shoes. "Haven't been doing that much anymore."

She checked her heels, then slipped them on, too. Straightened. "You're not interested? Or they're not?"

He stayed seated. "Both."

Silence fell. Was that a gleam of satisfaction and relief in her eyes? And what did it mean if it was? "What about you?" he asked curiously. "Dating anyone in particular?"

She went about the kitchen, tidying up unnecessarily. "Not that it's any of your business, but...no."

He watched the elegance of her moves. "Why not?" She was certainly gorgeous and accomplished enough to attract plenty of men. Not that he really wanted to see her go out with any of them...

She threw a damp paper towel into the trash. "Men are unreliable."

He tracked the movement of the golden heart pendant, visible in the V-neck of her cashmere sweater just above the hollow of her breasts. "Not all."

She met his eyes. Steady now. Resentful. "The ones I have been really interested in have been."

Funny, even though it had been years since they had dated, he could swear she was talking about him now.

Her phone chimed with an incoming text. She pulled it out of her pocket and frowned at the screen. Clearly unhappy.

The need to protect her was as strong as ever. "Everything okay?"

Her delicate brow furrowed. "I just got notice a package was delivered to me." She showed him the view from her front-door security camera.

He studied it, seeing nothing amiss. "And that's a problem because…?"

"I'm not expecting anything, never mind a package from Chef Express marked 'perishable.' I mean, what if it belongs to someone else, and it's their dinner, and they are waiting for it?"

Certainly possible. Feeling neighborly, too, he asked, "Want me to run over and pick it up for you?"

For a moment, he thought she was going to refuse, pretty much on principle. Then the reality of her situation seemed to dawn on her. She bit her lip. "Actually, that would be easier, if you wouldn't mind."

Anything to give him an excuse to spend more time with her. He winked. "Be back in a jiff," he promised before slipping out the door.

When Cade returned, ten minutes later, the girls had apparently finished straightening upstairs and were settled around the living room coffee table, playing a game of Candy Land.

They were so engrossed in what they were doing, they barely looked up as he carried the shipping box into the house for Allison. Seeing that it was indeed addressed to *her*, she frowned in confusion and waved him toward the kitchen.

Once there, she set the box on the breakfast room table. She cut through the clear package tape. Inside the cardboard box was a Styrofoam cooler with all the meal ingredients, along with a large gift envelope.

As she opened it and read the card, her expression was so stunned he couldn't help but ask, "Who is it from?"

"Laurel Grimes and Tripp Taylor, the executives from HITN."

The beneficiary of many such business gifts himself, he shrugged. "That's nice."

Her expression tightened with apprehension. "It's not a gift." She looked up at him. "This is my first *test* in the job interview process. They want to see how I operate under pressure. They're going to be contacting me in less than an hour, and they expect me to prepare the dinner in this box, in my cottage kitchen, while they simultaneously interview me via Skype."

Cade almost laughed, the notion was so ludicrous. Except it was no joke. She really was expected to do this. With very little notice, no less. Yet she already seemed up to the challenge. "You don't seem all that surprised by the request," he remarked.

Allison peered around the corner, checking to see if the girls were still well occupied with their board game. Reassured that they were, she returned to his side to continue talking to him in private. "Laurel

Grimes warned me...when we first started talking... that the competition for this slot was going to be fierce and I was going to have to prove myself, time and time again, if I wanted it." She shook her head amiably. "I guess this was what she meant."

He watched her look through the packets of meal ingredients and color-photo instructions. "What about the kids?"

Allison replaced the ice packs and put the top back on the cooler. "Well, normally I would just take them with me to my cottage if I had to do something for my work, but..."

He lounged against the counter, watching as Allison packed up her laptop computer, video equipment and camera. "It'd be a little hard to cook while answering questions during a Skyped job interview, and still keep an eye on them."

"Exactly," she murmured, sliding her cell phone into her shoulder bag. "In that sense...because I'm babysitting," she admitted ruefully, checking her watch, "this opportunity couldn't have come at a worse time."

And yet she was dealing with it, he noted with admiration.

She squared her slender shoulders, looked him in the eye and went on resolutely, "But the good news is you're here, and the girls apparently adore you, and you already wanted to be more involved this weekend. And Sarabeth and Shawn wanted that, too. So...

if you're still ready, willing and able to help watch them for a little bit, it's all good. Right?"

Pushing aside his private fear that her potential employer might already be asking way too much of her, he nodded. "Right."

Seeming to catch his reservations, she murmured reassuringly, "I don't think it's going to take more than two hours, max. Which means all you are going to have to do is watch over them and feed them dinner, and then I'll be back here in time to put the girls to bed. And get things ready for school tomorrow morning. So it should all be fine."

That wasn't really the point, he knew. She was setting a dangerous precedent with her potential new employer that would, if continued, leave her little boundary for a private life. He had lived that way with the Wranglers, giving every ounce of his energy to being the star pitcher and famous Texas "personality" they had needed and wanted him to be. No request was too big or too small; he had done them all. In the end, at great cost.

And it was no path to happiness.

Not that he expected she would listen to him if he tried to explain how the combination of unchecked ambition and celebrity could rob you of your soul. Never mind how hard it was to figure out who you really were at heart when the fame faded away, as all fame eventually did.

"Cade?" Misunderstanding the reasons behind

his apprehension, she said, "You already said you wanted to continue to help out this evening..." She looked at him peculiarly, as if wondering if she had gotten that wrong.

"And I will," he told her firmly. "I'll even ask one of my sisters to help out, just to make sure we have enough hands on deck. But are you sure this is the boundary you want to set with HITN, right out of the gate?"

She went into the mudroom and came back with her winter coat and scarf. "They were clear the job requires me to be flexible and able to rise to whatever the challenge of the moment happens to be."

Cade understood the unpredictability of work life, and performing well, no matter what the situation. He helped her with her coat while she put her arms in the sleeves.

Her eyes glittered with excitement. "And to make sure whomever they choose is up to the task, they will be giving both me and my competition a new challenge every day or so for the next week or two."

Well, that was *one* way to spend the Christmas holidays, Cade thought wryly.

She folded her pretty scarf in half, placed it around her neck and then slid the ends through the loop. "HITN will decide which one of us gets the new TV show based on our performance under pressure."

He had never seen her so amped up. Noticing a

section of her hair was caught in the scarf, he reached over to lift it free. The thick strands felt just as silky and feminine as he remembered.

Fingers tingling, he dropped his hand. "And you really, really want this," he guessed, wanting her to have her heart's desire, too.

Her grin widened. "I do."

Cade knew, from painful personal experience, that sacrificing literally everything for a job was the kind of mistake that could be very hard to come back from. But this wasn't his life, it was hers, so... "Then I'll do everything I can to help you," he promised.

For a moment, she looked a little surprised. As well as very touched. "Thank you!" Joy emanating from her, she moved into his arms and gave him an exultant hug.

The feel of her lithe body pressed warmly against his brought back so many memories. All of them good. Taking them right back into the past. When they'd still been together, and in that sense, so much happier. Before he knew it, he had given in to impulse and wrapped his arms around her, too.

Feeling zero resistance, he lowered his head. Her eyes closed. Then she drew in a soft, welcoming breath, and their mouths met.

Chapter Four

Allison knew she shouldn't be kissing Cade, never mind surrendering to the warm, sure pressure of his mouth in a way she never had before. But she couldn't help it. She was so happy and excited. So ready for more. In her life, her work and, most especially, her heart.

But that didn't mean he was the one for her now, she mused, as he cupped her face in his hands and ever so slowly deepened the kiss. Any more than he had been the one for her when they had broken up eight years before. And yet there was a part of her that wanted him as much as he seemed to want her, wanted to be as lost in him as she had ever been.

Had there not been four children on the premises and work for her to do, who knew what might have happened. But the responsibilities were there, and she was not as reckless with her heart as she once had been, so…

Hand to his chest, she wedged distance between them and tore her lips from his, pretending for the moment it was all his doing, when she knew just the opposite was true. Like bees and blossoms, when in close proximity, they could not stay away from each other. Which was why she had taken pains to stay out of his orbit for the last eight years. "Whoa there, slugger," she said.

Another mistake. *Slugger* had been the endearment she had used when they were together.

Feeling more guilty and aroused than ever, she flushed. "I'm sorry."

"For kissing me?" he asked in disbelief.

Ignoring the tingling of her body, Allison pulled herself together. "That shouldn't have happened. I let myself get carried away."

His sensual lips curved up at the corners. "Right." He clearly didn't believe her for one red-hot second.

Waving an airy hand, she cut him off with an indignant huff and took pains to clarify. "That was about the job. My excitement."

Another telltale lift of his dark brow. His gaze drifted over her lazily, lingering on the tautness of her breasts before leisurely cataloging her throat and face, returning to linger, even more seductively, on her eyes. "Oh, I got it," he drawled.

Which, of course, wasn't the way that sounded, either. Willing the desire welling inside her to go away, Allison slung her workbag over her shoulder and gathered up the shipping box she'd been sent, holding it in front of her like a shield. If only she hadn't felt the depth of his desire, too. "So, you'll be all right with the kids?"

He watched her, his expression inscrutable now, then reached for his phone. "I'll be great. Although—" Cade looked up from the text he was currently sending "—you may want to tell them what the new plan for the evening is before you go, so they aren't thrown off guard by the change in situation this evening."

Allison winced. What was wrong with her? The kids—not the job she was hoping to get—were supposed to be her main priority this evening!

She'd like to blame it all on Cade. But she knew she couldn't do that. For the first time in her life, her ambition was starting to get ahead of her. In ways she didn't particularly like. Was this the way it had been for Cade when he'd been aiming his sights on major-league baseball? And how ironic that the tables would now be turned and she would be the one with her priorities all out of whack…

Saying a silent apology for her momentary self-ishness, Allison forced herself to get back to the duties she had undertaken for the weekend, so that her exhausted, overworked friend might have a little time alone with her husband overseas while he got his big technology sales award.

"Of course." Determined not to let anyone down, she went to find the kids, who were still playing Candy Land in the living room with Zeus lounging nearby, watching them. The girls barely looked up as she explained she had a work thing she had to go do.

"Daddy is always going to work," Amber remarked, unsurprised.

"But he takes a suitcase," Jade added calmly.

"And his computer," Sienna supplied.

Allison patted her workbag, glad this felt normal to them. "I've got mine, too," she said. As well as her cameras.

"Are you going to be gone a bunch of days like he always is?" Hazel wanted to know.

Allison shook her head, beginning to feel guilty for deserting them and leaving them in Cade's capable hands. Even if it was only for a few hours. "No, I'll be back tonight, in time to help you get ready for bed. And here to see you off to school tomorrow morning."

The girls squinted at Cade, who had strolled in to join them, his expression still inscrutable. "Do you know how to order tacos?" Sienna asked.

"Because when Daddy makes dinner, he always gets us tacos and sopaipillas," Amber said.

Cade grinned. "I do," he said. "And not only that,

I have another surprise for you, because one of my sisters is coming over to have it with us!"

Clearly, he wasn't taking any chances, Allison thought, doing her best to become poker-faced, as well. "Thanks for stepping up," she said, admiring him for that.

He walked her to the door, then proceeded to carry the box to her car in a move that suddenly began to make it seem like a date. "Don't look so surprised."

Allison couldn't help it. In the past, their roles had been reversed. He had been the one always dashing off to do something to get ahead in his career. Now she was the one. And more surprising still, he was apparently okay with it.

"It's the new me," she said flippantly, then climbed behind the wheel and, aware the clock was ticking, drove away.

"Lovely presentation," Tripp Taylor, the programming director, said via Skype when Allison had finished making the entrée from the Chef Express home-meal service. The fit fiftysomething executive, with cropped silver hair and glasses, wore an open-collared shirt and blazer.

"Only one problem," the producer, Laurel Grimes, said. A decade younger than her boss, the pretty brunette was wearing a trendy silk shell top and fitted jacket.

Allison couldn't imagine what that would be, as she looked down at the two plates she had prepared. They were absolutely perfect.

"You added flourishes that weren't in the kit," Laurel said.

Allison blinked. "You mean the fresh herbs and the touch of cream and Dijon in the yogurt dill sauce?"

"As well as the lemon slices and freshly ground black pepper instead of the packaged pepper flakes that were enclosed," Tripp remarked, referring to his own copy of the cooking instructions included with the meal kit they had sent her.

Laurel nodded. "We need you to stick to the script, Allison. Adding additional ingredients makes it seem as if the dinners aren't okay on their own. Chef Express is never going to go for that. And since they are going to be a major sponsor for the new show, the show's host is going to have to understand and adhere to that."

"Of course." Allison could feel herself flushing in embarrassment. Why hadn't they given her a heads-up about that?

"Now, on to the branding," Tripp said.

The interview went downhill from there.

Fifteen minutes later, Tripp and Laurel told her they would be in touch with her new challenge soon. And that was that.

Aware time was wasting, Allison packed up the

two meals she had prepared and quickly loaded her dishes into the dishwasher. Taking the food with her, she headed out to her car and over to Sarabeth and Shawn's house.

Cade's sister Jillian was just getting ready to leave as Allison walked in. "Hey!" The botanist and antique rose expert engulfed her in a hug.

Jillian had helped Allison pick out the new landscaping for her cottage. And the truth was, Allison had always loved all of Cade's family. Luckily, none of them held their breakup against her.

Allison returned the hug, reveling in the sisterly affection. "Thanks for helping out with the girls tonight."

"Are you kidding?" Jillian stepped back, beaming. "I owe you, after all the business I got when you mentioned my roses on your blog postings."

"How could I not? They are the best in the state!"

They exchanged grins that reminded Allison how much she missed spending time with Cade's family. Pushing away the sudden wave of nostalgia, she drew a quick, enervating breath. "And speaking of the quadruplets…" She cast a glance around. "It's awfully quiet."

"They're asleep," Cade said.

"Already?" Allison set her bags on the foyer table and slipped out of her coat. "It's only seven thirty!"

He nodded, admitting, "They were exhausted."

"As well as messy after their dinner of tacos and

sopaipillas." Jillian laughed. "So I ushered them through their showers and into the pajamas while Cade did the dishes. Then we all sat down to listen to him read a story, and before he got to the end of *The Night Before Christmas*, their eyes were closing. So we tucked them in. And now," Jillian said, pulling on her own coat, "I really have to go because I have a date waiting for me."

So that was why she was wearing a skirt and sweater instead of her usual jeans. "Anyone special?"

"I won't know until I meet him." Jillian grinned. "It's a fix-up." She headed out.

Allison turned back to Cade, feeling a little bereft she had missed what sounded like a very nice evening with the girls. She had always thought she was happy not having kids, but now she was beginning to wonder if that were a mistake. If a happy life also meant having a very full life. Instead of one that was just well-ordered and peaceful.

"Do you think it would be okay for me to check in on them?" Allison asked. "I mean, I don't want to disturb them…" Especially when she had no idea how soundly they slept.

The tiniest smile played around the corners of his chiseled lips as he locked eyes with her. "I'm sure it will be fine." He touched her arm lightly. "I'll go with you." Quietly, they mounted the stairs. The dehumidifier made a soothing white noise in the hall. The girls' bedroom doors were all open. All four were indeed sound asleep. Amber was surrounded by so many stuffed zoo animals it was hard to see where she was in her bed. Jade was clutching one of the baby dolls they had intended to take swimming that afternoon. Sienna's loveys were scattered across the foot of her bed, and she was curled up on her side, grasping her pillow. Hazel was snuggling the Christmas elf and wearing a red-and-white-striped stocking cap much like the one they had seen in the storybook Cade had read them before bed.

"They look so sweet and peaceful," Allison whispered, as she backed out into the hall.

Cade nodded, clearly as touched as she. "Don't they," he murmured.

"Where is Zeus?"

Cade winced in chagrin. He motioned for her to follow, stopping a moment later in the doorway of Sarabeth and Shawn's bedroom. The black Lab had put himself to bed, too, in the tufted dog bed positioned at the foot of their four-poster bed. The pooch was snoring softly.

Allison's heart went out to the aging Labrador retriever. He'd had a heck of a day, too. She shook her head fondly. She'd never considered herself a dog person, but Zeus was making her doubt that attitude. "He's really out, too," she observed softly.

Looking relaxed and at ease, with his shirt open at the throat, his sleeves rolled up to just the elbow, Cade offered, "If you want me to wake him…"

Allison shook her head. The truth was, if the girls had a crisis, she might need him. "No. He can sleep here tonight."

She and Cade backed out of the room as soundlessly as they had come in. Chivalrously, he promised, "I'll come over first thing to feed and walk him, then."

Grateful for all his help, Allison smiled. "I would appreciate it."

They headed back down the stairs.

"Did you have dinner?" he asked.

She shook her head. The weariness from such a long, eventful day had her starting to drag a bit. "I assume you did."

"I figured I'd wait for you. Go and get you something if you hadn't eaten yet. Or—" he lifted one broad shoulder in an indolent shrug "—cook you something."

"You...cook?" When she'd known him, he'd been loath to spend any time in the kitchen if she was there to do it for him, which, when they'd been living together, she usually had been.

His gaze drifted over her appreciatively. He seemed to be contemplating putting the moves on her once again. "You'd be surprised what I can do these days," he murmured huskily.

May-be...

On the other hand, flirting with him was dangerous. How well she knew that. She forced herself to cut the repartee and be serious. Well mannered. After all, she owed him. If he hadn't helped her out tonight, she might not have been able to do the impromptu job interview. She adopted an impersonal tone. "I was going to eat some of the food I prepared. It made enough for two. So you're welcome to some…"

Even though she had yet to figure out a way to make herself immune to his charm.

"Sounds good," he said.

The heat of his smile made her tingle. "You don't know what we're having yet." There she went, teasing him again.

He followed her into the kitchen. "I remember how much I loved your cooking."

And she remembered how much she used to love him.

Cade studied the wistful expression on Allison's face. Something was clearly bothering her. "How did the interview go?" he asked. She'd been practically walking on air when she had rushed out of there. Now she seemed pensive at best.

Frowning, she got the covered containers out of the fridge. Began portioning food on two plates. "Not as well as I had hoped."

She put a plate into the microwave and pushed the dinner reheat button, then moved to get out the silverware.

His heart going out to her, Cade filled two glasses with ice and water. "In what sense?" he asked.

Allison used potholders to get the first plate out of the oven and set it on the island. She slid in the second plate, then turned the microwave back on. "Well, first of all, I screwed up the food-prep portion of the interview." Briefly, she explained.

Feeling she was being way too hard on herself, as usual, Cade soothed, "That's an easy fix. All you have to do is not deviate from the instructions and included ingredients next time."

Allison took the other plate out of the microwave and joined him at the island, taking the stool next to his. Her pretty green eyes were clouded with worry. "It's not just that." She ran her fork over the pan-seared salmon with dill cream sauce, fingerling potatoes and asparagus.

He took a bite and found the food as delicious as it looked. "I'm listening," he said gently.

"Well…" Seeming relieved to be able to unburden herself, she relayed, "Initially, because Jennifer Moore and I are both single thirtysomething lifestyle bloggers, it was really going to come down to small-town gal versus big-city woman."

"But it's more than that?"

"Jennifer's a real bachelorette. She makes no bones about the fact that she is looking for her Mr. Right, and if she finds him, plans to showcase her engagement, wedding and entry into newlywed life in her brand."

"Whereas you…"

"Want to show that a woman can be happy living the single life. That we don't have to be married or have kids to be content."

"And you incorporate that into your brand."

She lifted her glass to her lips, sipped slowly. "Yes."

"So it's really between the want-to-get-married audience and don't-want-to-get-hitched audience."

"Exactly."

She shifted on her stool and tugged the hem of her skirt down to her knees. The glimpse of silky thigh filled his body with need. Deliberately, he pushed the desire away.

Oblivious to the direction of his thoughts, Allison compressed her lips. "And they don't know which one is going to garner the best ratings right now. Which is why—" she sighed wearily "—they plan to do focus testing on both of our blogs, between now and the decision-making."

"And that will determine it," Cade guessed.

"Along with our flexibility and ability to handle stress." Allison looked as if she had the weight of the world on her slender shoulders. "They want to make sure they get someone who is ambitious but also easy to work with."

He reached over to cover her hand with his. "Then that should definitely be you."

She looked down at their entwined fingers. "Maybe."

It wasn't like her to be so doubtful. "Why wouldn't it be you?"

She withdrew her hand. Looking as if she had little appetite for the delicious food, she resumed eating. "Right now, most of their shows are hosted by married couples, or family of some sort."

He wasn't sure he understood.

"Two brothers. A mother and daughter. Two adult children and their dad," she explained.

"No one alone?"

"I'd be the first."

Assuming, Cade thought, she stayed as emotionally and romantically unattached as she planned.

She put her fork down. "Although I imagine they'd want to bring some community into it, to provide context."

Noting how pretty and feminine she looked in the soft light of the kitchen, Cade guessed, "But it would be more of a risk."

"Yes." She dabbed the corner of her lips with her napkin, stood and carried her plate to the sink. "And although my sense is that Laurel Grimes, the producer, is all about expanding the offerings to include lifestyle information, instead of just home decorating and renovation tips, Tripp Taylor, the programming director, seems more inclined to play it safe and just stick to what they know will work. Rather than take a risk on something that might not."

He joined her. "Like you."

She held his glance, seeming relieved that he was there. "Although it's true…I've got the handywoman aspect cornered, which meshes well with their existing programming, I'm not sure similarity will help me in this instance." Disappointment crept into her low tone. "Especially if single thirtysomething female viewers decide they would rather spend tons of money and hire people to do things for them, the way Jennifer Moore does, than do it themselves, the way I do."

"And I'm not sure a close comparison of your two life views won't work in your favor." Resolved to give her the comfort and consolation she needed, he took her in his arms. "Especially when potential fans see how sweet and smart and sensitive you are, and view your indefatigable, can-do spirit. Trust me," he said gruffly, as he noted the indecision in her pretty eyes. "When viewers get to know you, it's not going to be a contest." There was literally no way it could be.

The need to protect her growing by leaps and bounds, he drew her against him. Buried his face in her hair and inhaled her unique, sexy fragrance.

"Cade…" She caught her breath. Drew back enough to look up at him. Pink crept into her cheeks. As her gazed roved his face, she seemed every bit as ready to kiss him again as he was to kiss her. Yet she murmured, haltingly, "What happened this afternoon—"

He was done hiding his feelings. It had to be said. "Should definitely happen again."

Her body relaxed, as if in mute agreement, and he dropped his head for another kiss.

Allison hadn't let herself want anything outside her realm for a very long time. And yet she wanted Cade, she acknowledged, as she wound her arms around his neck, opened her mouth to the plundering pressure of his and let her body soften against him. He was her Achilles' heel. In more ways than one. Which was why she couldn't let him turn her perfectly ordered world upside down. Not again. Not when his own life was in flux.

Trembling, she tore her mouth from his, stepped back. "We can't do this." Couldn't begin to need each other again in ways that could not easily be undone. At least not for her.

He went still. "It was just a kiss." Tenderness and understanding radiated in his gaze.

Their second in one day.

Allison ran her hands through her hair. "To you, maybe." She forced herself to explain, "To me, it's a pathway to unhappier times."

He frowned in regret. "I'm sorry for the way I treated you back then." His gaze drifted over her lovingly, his mood as quietly accepting as hers was troubled and pensive. "The way I took you for granted."

I'm sorry, too. Being completely alone with him, without the girls as a shield, was proving more challenging than she had expected.

Allison squared her shoulders defiantly. Lifted her chin. "Then you should understand why I would never want to go back to that. Especially when you and I both know that this is just because you're at loose ends."

He stood, looking over at her, hands braced on his waist. "You really think I'd put the moves on you because I was bored?"

What other reason could there be? It wasn't as if they were still in love, or ever would be again. Resolved to do what was best for both of them, Allison resurrected the barriers around her heart. Stepping closer, she reminded him kindly, "You had two pitching injuries this year. The second forced you to retire years earlier than you expected. And pretty much broke your athlete heart. That was only four months ago."

He gave her a long look that spoke volumes about all the issues he had yet to work through. "And your point is?"

She pulled in a stabilizing breath, clasped her hands in front of her and tried again. "Your life is in turmoil. You don't even know what you want to pursue next."

"That's not true," he said, leaning toward her. And

with an even more intimate look, he said, "I know *exactly* what I want to do next."

"Then tell me," Allison said.

Chapter Five

Just because Cade knew exactly what he wanted to do next did not mean he was ready to share. "It's in the early stages."

Allison's delicate brow furrowed. "Uh-huh."

She didn't believe him, so he offered proof. "It was why I was wearing a sport coat and tie when I came over earlier."

"I'm listening."

He shrugged affably. "That's all I'm prepared to say right now."

Her lower lip slid out into a delectable pout. "And once again, we're on uneven ground."

He watched her storm over to the sink and wash

her hands, then bring the makings for the next day's lunches out of the fridge. "What is that supposed to mean?" He washed his hands, too.

She lined up eight pieces of bread on the cutting board with more than necessary concentration. "I told you what my career aspirations were. I even confessed my uncertainty about what the results might eventually be." She looked up long enough to glare at him. "You won't tell me anything."

He stood on one side of the island and opened up the package of provolone cheese. "I don't want to jinx it."

She stood on the other side and got out the turkey. "So it has something to do with being an athlete."

"An ex-athlete," he corrected, as they each doled out four slices.

She handed him the raspberry jelly and a knife. Not sure what he was supposed to do with that, he gave her an odd look. She flushed, explaining, "It's how they like it. So just put a little on each sandwich."

Hmm. He never would have thought to try that. "Okay."

Allison got out a cucumber and a small cutting board and knife, and began julienning it into kid-sized strips. "Are you going to do more commercials?"

As always, her motions were delicate and precise. Trying not to wonder if she was just as delicate and precise when she made love these days, he cut all four sandwiches into triangles and put them into Ziploc plastic bags. "All my endorsements ended when my tenure at the Wranglers did."

She portioned the cucumber into four snack containers. Slid those, and individual containers of ranch dressing, into the lunch sacks. "Is that why you sold your home in Dallas? Because you could no longer afford it?"

He added the sandwiches. "No. I've got plenty of money socked away for a rainy day." He had always been smart about that. As was she.

She added individual containers of applesauce and plastic spoons, closed the tops and put them all into the fridge.

"I just wanted to come home," he said, as she turned to face him. "Be in Laramie County again."

Her expression gentled. For a moment, she just stood there, leaning against the fridge, her hands splayed on either side of her. "I felt the same way after my mom died," she admitted softly. "It's why I returned, too."

He let his gaze rove over her, aware all over again how pretty she was, even at the end of a very long day with her hair mussed. "Because you wanted to live here."

Unable to be still, even for a minute, she brushed past him into the laundry room. "Not at first." She bent down to open up the extra-large capacity clothes dryer, giving him a very nice view of her exquisite derriere as she pulled out a dozen or so towels. Then she proceeded to pile the clean dry linens onto the folding table that stretched over top of the dual machines.

She started to fold. He moved in to stand beside her and help.

"Initially, I just intended to fix up her house the way she would never let me when she was alive."

Catching a whiff of her jasmine perfume, Cade sympathized, "I remember your mom was pretty frugal."

"Very frugal. Hence, the decor being stuck back in the 1970s when she bought it. Anyway, I needed some time to myself to grieve, and I needed to be in a safe, comforting place, so I quit my interior design job in Dallas and headed home."

She flashed him a wan smile as they folded. "I started blogging so my friends could see what I was up to. Former clients followed me as well, and before I knew it, I had a lot of people liking it and checking in daily."

Including me, Cade thought.

"So I picked up some advertisers for the how-to videos I made and turned it into a business. And now here I am." She bowed facetiously. "Doing what I probably should have been doing all along."

"Well, if all goes well, the same will soon be true for me," he said.

She treated him to a withering glare. "You're still not going to tell me?"

Silence stretched out between them, increasing the tension. It was either jinx it or have her mad at him for holding out on her. Easy to decide which won. Exhaling, he revealed, "Coach Jenkins is looking to retire at the end of January."

A mixture of recognition and something that might have been approval lit her green eyes. "The baseball coach at the high school," she mused softly.

Cade nodded, not sure why he wanted her in his corner, just knowing he did. "I want his job," he stated plainly.

"Well—" Allison lifted her hand airily, her emotions suddenly seeming more mixed up than ever "—then of course you will get it."

He hated it when she pretended something was settled when it definitely was not. "Well, actually, I may not," he countered grumpily.

She gave him a look that spoke volumes. "Cade, if anyone knows baseball, it's you. Plus, you're naturally good with kids. They'd be lucky to have you."

Cade had thought so, too, when he had heard about the job opening up. He grabbed another towel. "Coach Jenkins isn't sure I'd be a good role model."

Allison shot him a look over her slender shoulder. "Because of all the star player behavior?"

Cade nodded. "The women, the clubbing…"

Allison scoffed, looking resentful again. He wondered how much of the celebrity gossip she believed. And, more important, what it would take to redeem himself in her eyes.

"You can hardly blame him," she said, adding to the stack of linens with unnecessary force.

He grabbed the next-to-last towel. Moving slower now. "It wasn't as glamorous as it looked."

Allison took the last towel. "Tell that to teenage boys trying to make college teams. Heading down the same path."

"Exactly." He might have ruined it for himself in this sense, too. Not because he had done most of what had been alleged about him, but because he hadn't done enough, in terms of his own behavior, to correct the public record. And wouldn't that suck, if his own inaction then cost him what he wanted now? With the job. With Allison...

Finished, Allison leaned against the laundry room wall, her arms folded in front of her. "So what are you going to do?" she asked gently.

Figuring this was as good a place to talk as anywhere, Cade lounged opposite her. "Put together a whole list of references that show all the volunteering and mentoring I did that wasn't in the news."

She studied him, looking very much like the girl he'd fallen in love with, lo those many years before. "Because you didn't want it to be."

Wishing he could kiss her again, and have it not taken the wrong way, Cade shrugged. "Well, you know what they say. If anyone else knows about it, it isn't really charity. It's grandstanding."

Another silence fell, shorter this time. "Are you sure you'll be happy here in such a small town?" She squinted at him, considering. "That you won't get bored back in rural Texas?"

With you here? Cade thought. *Not a chance.*

"I'm sure." Able to see she didn't believe him, he promised before taking his leave, "And one day you'll be certain of that, too."

"I'm so glad I caught you," Sarabeth told Allison over FaceTime the next morning. "This seven-hour time difference is impossible!"

Although she had never been in Switzerland, Allison sympathized. "It looks like you're about to head out to dinner." And a fancy one at that. Sarabeth was wearing a dazzling evening gown. Shawn, a tuxedo.

"The awards presentation is this evening." Sarabeth appeared even more stressed out than she had when they'd left Texas. "And then there's a dance after that, so…"

Shawn came into the picture. "We probably won't be back to our suite until after the girls are asleep. So we'll call and FaceTime with them tomorrow morning, if that's okay, since there is no school on Saturday."

"I'm sure they would love that," Allison said.

"How are they doing?" Sarabeth asked. "Are you able to handle them on your own?"

"Actually," Allison admitted, pausing as Cade walked in the back door with the family Lab on a leash, "the girls missed Zeus, so Cade brought him over for a visit yesterday afternoon, and he has been pitching in quite a lot, too." He had come over, as promised, to feed and walk Zeus that morning, so she could concentrate on everything else that had to be done.

"Good." Pleased, Shawn turned to his wife. "See? I told you there was nothing to worry about. Allison and Cade have this covered. The girls will be fine until we get back."

"I know." Sarabeth sighed in frustration. "But it's the first time I've ever been away from the quadruplets since they were born. And it's hard for me," she finished, clearly piqued her husband didn't understand.

Shawn exhaled. "I miss them, too, Sarabeth. The difference is I think we should still have a life."

Sensing a quarrel coming on, one that had been going on for quite a while now, Allison plastered a breezy smile on her face. "Well, we're going to let you two go now. But have fun this evening, and congrats on your award, Shawn!"

"And don't worry about anything here," Cade reassured them kindly. "Because we've got this."

The couple thanked them, and the call concluded.

Sighing, Allison put her phone down. "I was hoping they'd really relax and enjoy themselves," she murmured, concerned.

Cade's lips compressed as he ran a hand through his hair. Instead of his usual athletic clothes, he was dressed like a cowboy in a thermal tee that buttoned halfway down the front and a flannel shirt, jeans and boots. She could tell that he'd showered, but he hadn't shaved, and the day's growth of beard gave him a ruggedly sexy look. "There's still time for that to happen," he predicted.

"Maybe," Allison said, inhaling the unique masculine scent of him. "So what are you up to today?" she asked curiously.

The way his eyes twinkled indicated he appreciated her interest. "I'm going out to the ranch to help my dad put up the exterior Christmas lights. I'll take Zeus with me."

She watched him unsnap the dog's leash and fill the water bowl for him. "That's nice of you."

Finished, he straightened. "We were going to do it tomorrow, but I moved it to today so I'd be around to help you with the girls this weekend when they aren't in school."

She met his gaze gratefully, no longer too proud to say, "I'd appreciate that."

He touched her shoulder briefly. "In the meantime, I'll bring Zeus by after school, so they can see him."

Ignoring the tingling deep inside her, she drew a breath. "Great."

"And maybe we can figure out something Christmassy to keep them busy, so they're not so out of control?"

That was Cade. Always thinking ahead. She smiled, wishing she had the time to just go and hang out with them today. "I'll see if I can come up with something," she promised.

"Sounds good." He gave her another long look, for a moment seeming to feel as reluctant to say goodbye as she did. But that was ridiculous. It wasn't as if this were a date or anything. Or would even lead to one. They were co-babysitters, that was all. And drafted ones at that.

Allison put aside the desire to kiss him goodbye. Or at the very least give him a hug. "Well, I've got to go back to my place and work on a new blog posting."

He held the door for her, locked up, and then he and Zeus walked her as far as her car. "Any special tasks from HITN?" he asked casually, his manner warm and supportive.

For a second, she let herself lean on him again before she put herself in work mode. "Not yet, but as they say, the day is young." Who knew what would happen for either her or Cade before it ended?

It took five minutes to get to her cottage, and five minutes after that, she received the second task from the network. A holiday card featuring a photo of her home instead of family.

Luckily, it was something fairly easy to accomplish, and by two o'clock that afternoon, Allison had posted the greeting card bearing the photo of the gorgeous wreath on her front door under the What's New This Holiday! banner on her website.

Relieved that was done, she began packing up what she needed to keep the girls busy after school. She was nearly finished when her doorbell rang.

Somehow, she wasn't surprised to see Cade and Zeus on her front steps. "Hey. Saw you were still here and wondered if you needed help picking up the girls from pre-K."

Her pride had her wanting to say, "No. I've got this."

However, the previous day's experience had her ushering them into her cottage instead. It was the first time he had been in the home she had been raised in since they'd broken up.

"Wow," he said.

She flushed with pride as he looked around. Taking in the places where walls had been removed to allow for an open-concept living area on the first floor, with beautifully finished pine floors. The kitchen sported new stainless appliances, navy kitchen cabinets, open shelving and pristine white marble countertops, as well as an island sized exactly right for the space. She also had an antique table for four beside the bay windows in the breakfast room. And a cozy cream-colored L-shaped sofa, dressed with pastel throws and pillows, formed a conversation area in front of the pale rose brick fireplace.

"I mean, I saw the photos on your blog," Cade continued, admiring the newly rebuilt open staircase to the second floor, "but they don't do it justice. This is really, really nice," he noted sincerely. "Very you."

Allison beamed. She didn't know why his approval mattered so much, only that it did. "Thank you!"

"Your mom would be impressed."

She petted Zeus's head, then watched him make himself at home and walk over to lie down next to the hearth. "I hope so. Although she was never one for decorating."

"That doesn't mean she wouldn't still be proud of you."

True.

He looked at the box on her kitchen island with cookie cutters, a rolling pin and baking sheets. "Is this for the kids?"

She nodded as the doorbell rang again.

"Expecting someone?" he asked.

Allison shook her head. Hoping it wasn't another meal kit from HITN, she headed for the door.

On the other side of the portal was a statuesque blonde in a dove-gray cashmere coat, sophisticated sweater and slacks. Model pretty, perfectly made-up, she had a large holiday gift basket in hand with a card bearing the *City Lights* logo.

"Hello, Allison. I'm your competition, Jennifer Moore," she said.

"All the way from Dallas." Allison was stunned to find that the social influencer looked even more like Nicole Kidman than she did in the photos on her blog.

Jennifer pressed the gift into Allison's hands. "I thought we should meet. And I wanted to wish you the best of luck."

"Thank you!" Allison said cheerfully, wishing she'd thought to do the same. "Best of luck to you, too!" Exercising her best Texan hospitality, she opened the door wide. "Won't you come in?"

"Love to." Jennifer stepped across the threshold, waiting while Allison set the basket on the foyer table and shut the door behind her, then turned to Cade, who was standing there with Zeus at his side. There was no question she recognized him, Allison thought. And she sized him up with the ease of someone used to mingling with the rich and famous. "Cade Lockhart!" Jennifer smiled sweetly. "How's that pitching arm these days?"

Allison was pleased to note that Cade seemed unfazed by her dazzling beauty. "Retired," he said dismissively.

"I would ask how you two knew each other—"

Jennifer waved an airy hand "—but my research showed you used to date."

Research? Allison had taken a cursory look at the other woman's website and social media when she had heard they were both in the running for the same slot. She hadn't tried to pry into the other woman's private life. Present or past. But maybe that spoke to her naivete rather than the other woman's intentions, which at the moment were still a little unclear.

"Can I get you something?" she asked, determined to keep this competition civil.

Jennifer continued looking around, taking in the newly decorated interior. Her expression indicated she found the cozy-cottage style with the touch of rustic elegance all rather pedestrian. "Do you have… um…hmm…" She tilted her head as if searching for something that might be available out in this "provincial" small Texas town. "Tap water?" she finally asked in a mildly condescending tone.

If that was the best she could do with thinly veiled insults, Allison thought, it wasn't much. While beside her, Cade snorted softly. It was all she could do not to elbow him in the ribs. "As well as sparkling and flavored," she retorted with a nervous laugh, still using her best manners. Surely, this woman hadn't driven two and a half hours just to try to intimidate her!

Jennifer wrinkled her nose, then said finally, "Actually…I think I'll pass." She paused as if tamping down her worst instincts, then leaned in conspir-atorially and sighed. "I just wanted to tell you not to feel *too bad* when this is all over."

So she *was* here to bully her! *Nothing like having an agenda.* Allison did what she always did when ini-tially confronted by a mean girl—she played dumb. "Why would I feel bad?" she asked, mirroring the other woman's faux innocence.

Jennifer's cool eyes narrowed. "I hate to say it, sugar, but I've got this locked up."

Well, clearly Laurel Grimes didn't think so. Feeling her own temper beginning to flare, Allison folded her arms in front of her and asked, "If that's the case, then why are they interviewing me?"

"Honestly, I don't know," Jennifer cooed, still pre-tending she was on Allison's side in all this. "It's *such* a waste of time and energy. And, of course—" she shook her head in wordless lament "—they're getting your hopes up *only* to have to break your heart."

Cade's jaw set and his eyes went flinty. "You must really want this," he observed.

And then some, Allison thought, glad for Cade's unwarranted protectiveness.

Seeming to realize she had met an unmovable wall in Cade, Jennifer sobered. "I do," she confided. Then, turning back to Allison, she regarded her rival staunchly. "Which is why I'm not going to let anything—or anyone—get in my way."

Cade stepped closer to Allison and wrapped a strong arm about her shoulders, his warmth and strength encompassing her like a thick blanket on a cold winter's day. "Now, Jennifer," he drawled, his voice dripping with disdain as he drew Allison in even closer against his side, "I'm sure you didn't mean it that way, but that does sound like a threat."

This time, Allison did elbow him lightly in the side. First of all, she was quite capable of defending herself. Even if she was secretly enjoying him going all caveman on her. Second of all, just because her competitor was unnecessarily aggressive did not mean they had to sink to her level.

Jennifer Moore gave Cade a look that said, one, she did not understand why he was not immediately slayed by her incredible sophistication and beauty, and two, she really wished he would stay out of this. "It's advice," she counseled sagely, looking him hard in the eye, then whipping her glance back over to Allison. "Walk away now, sugar, and you'll still be able to grow your little brand, down-home Texas as it is. Don't, and, well—" she shrugged and tossed her luxuriant mane "—the truth has a way of coming out. Especially when it comes to a person's *authenticity*. And that can be oh so embarrassing!" She paused to let her words sink in before wheeling around and heading for the door.

* * *

Allison watched the other woman leave, with a mixture of confusion and resentment.

Cade's gaze skimmed her face. "What the heck is she talking about?" he asked curiously. "Why would she think you, of all people, weren't authentic?"

Trying to take what had just happened in stride, she attempted a casual attitude she couldn't begin to feel. "I have no idea."

Trying to decipher the cryptic message, Allison searched her brain for possibilities. What could possibly undermine the successful-single style she had worked so hard to cultivate? Never mind her decision never to pursue romantic love again after the end of her eight-year relationship with Cade. Because what really was the hope she would ever find the kind of all-encompassing, all-giving love she yearned for? She had given everything she had to making her relationship with Cade work. Sacrificed until not a single one of her own needs were met. While he had completely taken her for granted. Part of that was her fault, of course. She hadn't told Cade how she was feeling. She had just expected him to notice and make amends. He never had. Not until she was past the point of ever forgiving him for his cavalier attitude.

It hadn't been easy, breaking up with him, though. Not when she was so used to them being a couple, albeit an increasingly unhappy one.

But, unlike her widowed mother, who had never really adjusted to life on her own, Allison had known her life could be better. Even without a man in it. And she had made the decision to *embrace* instead of *lament* her singleness and celebrate her ability to do whatever she wanted, how she wanted, when she wanted.

As well as encourage other independent-minded women to do the same. By creating happiness in every way and buying a home—or, in her case, *inheriting* one—and fixing it up with panache instead of waiting for some man to come along and do it for you.

"Unless—" the next possibility hit Allison with destabilizing force "—she's talking about my childhood."

Cade's brow furrowed.

Allison sighed, thinking of the stark contrast between then and the outward trappings of success she had worked so very hard to earn and enjoy now. With a sigh, she explained, "I guess she could be calling me a fraud because, unlike her—who, according to her blog postings has apparently always had wealth and lived a certain way—I haven't."

Aware Cade still didn't get it, Allison continued, "She could be referencing the five or six years after my dad died. When I was in elementary school and money was so tight, and the paint was falling off the cottage. My mom and I had to buy our clothing at the secondhand stores." Even at a young age, she had been able to feel the humiliation that came with being proud and poor. And wanted instead for everything to be enviably nice, the way they were for her now.

"I don't remember that," Cade said, frowning.

Allison was glad. "By the time you moved to Laramie County, I was in middle school, and my mom had a job as a secretary. So things weren't great, but they were better. And we were finally able to get the exterior of the house painted."

"But you never did anything much to the interior back then," he recalled, referencing the worn-out furniture and appliances, and wallpaper so old and ugly it was yellowed with age.

"No. Although I found out when my mom passed, and saw how much she had in savings, that she certainly could have lived a lot more comfortably."

Cade took her hand and led her over to sit on the sofa next to him. "Why didn't she, then?"

Allison relaxed into the curve of his arm. Realizing she probably did need to talk about this, she admitted, "I think my mom was just afraid after barely being able to hang on to the house after my dad died. She didn't want to be living hand to mouth ever again and the only thing that made her feel safe was having as much as possible set aside."

He nodded, understanding. "I felt the same way after foster care. I wanted money...lots of it..."

"The kind you get playing major-league baseball," Allison guessed, loving his warmth and his strength.

He tightened his grip on her hand. "It seemed like the only way."

"Except, unlike my mom," she teased, "you spent a lot of yours."

"Yeah, well—" he grinned, apparently not really regretting the flashy cars he'd bought and the lavish vacations he'd taken "—I also wanted to enjoy every day to the fullest."

Another thing that bonded them. "Same here." Allison smiled. "Which is why my blog celebrates being happy on your own and giving yourself the nicer things in life."

Even though she secretly wished sometimes that her life had turned out differently. That she'd been able to find her happily-married-ever-after.

But she also knew after eight years in a relationship with Cade, the man who had always felt like the one love of her life, that if they hadn't worked out, no other union likely would, either…

Cade misunderstood the source of the worry behind her frown. "Maybe that's why Jennifer Moore feels so threatened by you," he said.

Threatened?! Allison turned to better see his face, her leg inadvertently brushing up against his. "You think that was behind her visit?"

Protectiveness came and went in his expression. She had the feeling he wanted to pull her all the way onto his lap and hold her close, but also had the common sense not to take them back to a time when heartbreak had been the prevailing emotion between them. "One hundred percent," he said in a gruff-tender voice that sent shivers ghosting over her skin.

Suddenly realizing how easy it would be to lean on him and find herself in his arms again, Allison forced herself to focus on the one thing that had mattered to her in the years since she and Cade had split up. Her blossoming career.

"Well, I don't care what her motive was. I am not going to let her intimidate me. I'm going to win this thing, no matter what it takes."

Cade hoped that wasn't the case.

Mostly because he knew better than anyone that unchecked ambition could lead to poor decision-making...and unimaginable sorrow...when outside pressures trumped one's lifelong dreams.

He also knew that just because he had screwed up his life, professionally, out of a desire to succeed no matter what the obstacle, it did not mean that Allison would do the same.

Of the two of them, she had always been the more practical. He had to believe, for both their sakes, that that was still the case.

"So what's next?" he asked, forcing himself to put his worry aside.

Allison checked the time, all relaxed efficiency

once again. Rising, she headed for the kitchen, Zeus at her heels. "We pick up the girls at school and go back to their house and make cookies."

We. Cade liked the sound of that. He also knew Allison was quite the perfectionist when it came to her baking. "Does that mean Zeus and I get to help cook?" he teased. "Or will we just be around for the cleanup?"

She laughed. "Are you kidding? We want you both there from start to finish." Allison leaned down to scratch Zeus behind the ears. Then looked at Cade and smiled. "The girls and I wouldn't have it any other way."

Chapter Six

Four hours later, the spicy scent of freshly baked gingerbread and rich vanilla buttercream filled the Bailey kitchen. "Mr. Cade, you are terrible at this!" Jade said.

Her face dotted with equal parts flour and confectioners' sugar, Amber pointed at the gingerbread Santa made out of dough. "It's all wrinkly!"

"If you put it on the pan like that," Sienna told him critically, "we won't even be able to tell what it is!"

Hazel giggled and gave the only guy in the room a sympathetic look. "Santa's face is kind of lumpy!"

Cade shot Allison an apologetic look that only she could see, then turned his attention back to the quadruplets. "You're all right." Cade sighed, spatula filled with half an unbaked cookie still in hand. "It is a problem."

Able to see an intervention was needed, Allison eased in. Had it been any other man doing such a bad job, she would have assumed he was messing up on purpose to get out of what had turned into a four-hour marathon, with only a brief break for a pizza dinner. But Cade had been trying his best. Up to now, fairly successfully.

She put her hand over his wrist and felt the tension in his forearm that did not appear to be in the rest of his body. Maybe because this was his pitching arm, the one he'd had a second arthroscopic surgery on just a few months prior. "Allow me?"

His big body relaxed and he dipped his head in obvious relief. "Be my guest."

Happy to help him out the way he'd been aiding her, she eased the dough back onto the board. Patted it gently into the original shape. "It's still lumpy," Jade said.

Allison agreed. She also knew the girls were on the verge of becoming crabby with fatigue. "We'll just reroll out this small section of dough. But the rest can go on the cookie pan, I think." The oven timer buzzed, and she looked over at Cade. "Can you get that for me?"

"Sure." He grabbed a mitt and went to the wall oven. The pan was halfway out when he hissed unexpectedly and it tilted downward a good forty-five degrees. Somehow, he managed to get the baking sheet over to the ceramic stovetop to cool without dropping it entirely. But several cookies slid off in the process, splatting as they hit the floor. Zeus, who had been resting nearby, looked over with interest.

"Don't even think about it, buddy," Cade warned, using the mitt to pick up the ruined treats. He set the broken pieces on the stove next to the pan. "We don't want you burning your mouth."

Zeus put his head back down.

In unison, the girls frowned at Cade, clearly not understanding what the problem was. "You ruined some of our cookies, Mr. Cade!" Jade scolded.

"That's not nice!" Amber's lower lip slid out petulantly.

"I agree." Allison stepped in. "Mr. Cade!" she declared with enough drama to make him grin. She grabbed the swell of bicep on his uninjured arm. "You're going to have to sit down." She guided his big resisting form toward one of the breakfast-table chairs.

Realizing what she was up to, Cade dragged his feet. "I can still help," he insisted stubbornly.

"Nope. I'm putting you in time-out!" Allison declared, playing it up in order that the ruined cookies would be all but forgotten.

He let his jaw drop and played out his part in return. "No fair, Miss Allison!" He pouted.

The girls began to giggle.

"You're clearly overtired," Allison said, wagging her finger in his handsome face.

The girls giggled even more.

Cade folded his arms in front of him and thrust out his lower lip defiantly. Feeling guilty she hadn't recognized he was suffering discomfort sooner, Allison crossed her own arms and glared back. "How long do I have to sit here?" he asked.

Until your arm feels better, Allison thought. "Five minutes. In the meantime…" She turned to the girls, stunned at how long it had taken just to get as far as they had, with two dozen cookies completely decorated and two more dozen merely baked. Never mind how much mess they had made, with flour and frosting and bits of dough clinging to the island and floor and cabinet fronts. "I think it's time for you all to clean up and get ready for bed."

Surprisingly, they didn't argue with her. "Can Mr. Cade read us a story tonight?" Sienna asked gleefully.

"I want to hear *Llama Llama Holiday Drama*!" Hazel said.

Allison sent him a questioning look. An affable grin deepened the crinkles around his eyes. "I'm up for that." And so much more, it seemed.

"Sounds perfect," she said.

"Girls asleep?" Cade asked fifteen minutes later.

Allison nodded, glad they were at the point where

she could concentrate on just him instead of four girls, a dog and a baking project that had turned out to be way too complicated for their age group. "Almost before their heads hit the pillows. Zeus is upstairs, too, on his cushion, snoring away."

Cade rose from the sofa. She noticed his cheeks were slightly ruddy, which could have been from the time he had spent working outside with his dad that morning, but the rest of his face was pale in the way that usually signaled pain.

"Poor guy," he declared huskily, as he followed her into the kitchen. "It was a long day for him."

"I know." Allison motioned for Cade to sit on one of the stools. When he did, she went to the pantry. Emerging with a Ziploc plastic bag, she went straight to the freezer. Able to feel his gaze on her, she began filling the gallon bag with ice. "It was a long day for you, too."

As she turned, she saw he had his flannel shirt off and was trying to ease off the thermal T-shirt, as well. Which wasn't easy, since he seemed to be having difficulty raising his injured shoulder enough to free it. "And you need to let me do that!"

Worried he would hurt himself all the more, she brought the ice back to him, then helped him get the shirt all the way off. Which left him bare-chested. A situation that would be perfect for the proper application of ice. Not so perfect for her, however, when she was trying hard not to be so physically attracted to him. She swallowed at the sight of all that satiny-smooth skin on his broad shoulders and muscular back, the strip of dark hair that covered the center of his chest and arrowed down into the waistband of his jeans. Which wouldn't have been so bad had she not known from personal experience just how magnificently built the rest of him was.

Oblivious to the reason behind her discomfiture, he caught her hand before she could apply the bag of ice. He searched her face. "Why do you have to do this?"

Their fingers brushed as she reluctantly handed it over to him. "Because you're obviously in pain, silly."

He scoffed, all virile man. "How do you know?"

She noticed he didn't outright deny it. Which was good. She met and held his gaze. "By the poor way you handled a spatula and nearly dropped the cookie sheet at the end."

"Okay. You win. My shoulder hurts like the dickens."

"You should have mentioned it earlier."

"I didn't want to put a damper on the fun." His lips set. "Does Sarabeth have any tape, do you know?"

Allison went to the catchall drawer. There in the back was a big roll of bright blue masking tape. She held it up for him to see. "Will this do?"

"Yes." He looped the bag of ice over his rotator cuff and then drew out a long piece of tape. She held the bag in place for him while he secured it. She hadn't done this for him in years, and the action brought back a lot of memories, most of them good.

What would it have been like had they stayed together all these years instead of split up? Would they be as quarrelsome as Shawn and Sarabeth? Or would they have found a way to come together, in harmony, the way they had the past two days? Allison sighed. Why was she suddenly looking back? She had put their romantic past behind them. Or she *thought* she had, until he had kissed her again and stirred up all the deliberately forgotten feelings.

Now that he had gotten the ice in place, she went to get his flannel shirt. She held it out so he could slip his good arm into the sleeve. Then she draped the rest around his broad shoulders and brought the fabric down over his chest, covering as much as she could.

"Are you in this much pain a lot?"

He settled farther back on the stool, his long legs braced on either side of him. "Almost never."

"Why today, then? Is it due to all the activity at the ranch, helping your dad? Or your torn rotator cuff and subsequent surgeries?"

Cade's eyes darkened. "Probably both," he admitted, scowling. "And what do you know about the latter?"

She had never liked it when he put her on the spot like this. She rummaged around in the cupboard until she found the first-aid kit, then brought out small bottles of ibuprofen and acetaminophen. He took three tablets from the first.

She handed him a glass of water, aware he was still waiting for her to answer.

Shrugging, Allison met his gaze equably. "All I know is what I read in the news and heard on the grapevine here."

"Which was what?" he probed.

She moved to make him a cup of coffee, in the Keurig, knowing that hot liquid would help the medicine he had just taken dissolve and absorb faster. "You got hurt, pitching."

He studied her, guessing correctly that she had kept up with his life and career a lot more than she would like to let on. "Mmm-hmm." His attention drifted to her lips before returning with slow deliberation to her eyes. "What else?" He caught the filled mug she pushed at him, wordlessly shaking his head no when she gestured at the cream and sugar. Then searched her face.

Pulse accelerating, Allison concentrated on making a cup of coffee for herself and remained silent.

He moved into her sight line. "Tell me." He cupped the mug between his hands, but lifted it to his mouth with his uninjured arm.

She stirred cream and sugar into her decaf. Then, figuring it was best he get off his feet, she grabbed the plate of cookies and moved to sit beside him.

Maybe it was time she heard his side of the story. "There was gossip on some of the blogs that cover the Wranglers."

He listened, his eyes gleaming with undecipherable emotion.

She handed him a cookie and took one for herself, too. "Apparently, some of the sportswriters talked to the Wranglers' general manager, who hinted that the end of your career was all your fault, because you took an unnecessary risk coming back too soon."

He continued to study her with his steady gaze, as if trying to figure something out. "I'm sure the GM would say that."

"You didn't get along with him."

His powerful body tensed and he oozed testosterone. "Not at the end, no."

Her heart skittered in her chest. "Why not? I mean, you get along with everyone."

"It's complicated."

Aware it was going to be very hard to really get to know who he was now, if he didn't willingly confide in her, Allison drew a breath. She refused to get sucked in by the blatant sexiness of his gaze. "I understand complicated," she told him quietly. "But if you don't want to talk about it, if you don't want us to be all that close, I understand that, too."

To Cade's surprise, he wanted her to know the whole sordid story. Maybe because he knew she was the one person on this earth who would understand why he had acted the way he had.

Knowing the only way to ease the throbbing in his shoulder was to try to relax while the ice did its trick, he took her by the hand and led her into the living room and settled with her on the sofa. Keeping her palm in his, he gave her the recap of events. "The Wranglers had a good year and were headed for the playoffs, but they needed all their pitchers back if they were going to make it past the division championship."

She toed off her flats and tucked her black tights-clad legs beneath her. "Especially you, because you were their very best."

Unable to help noting how feminine and delicate her hand was, he turned her palm over, resting it on his thigh, and traced the lifeline with the pad of his thumb. "Right."

"But you were still recovering from your first surgery."

He nodded, loving the intent way she always listened to him. "I was also itching to go back. I'd been out for months. I wanted to play. The problem was, I knew the team doctors weren't going to green-light me just yet. But I also had the option to choose my own physician, and—" this was the hard part "—it was suggested to me if I went to a certain Fort Worth orthopedist, she would give me the okay. And that if she did, Wranglers management would look the other way and accept her decision."

Allison paled. "Even though she shouldn't have said you were ready to play again?"

Cade wasn't about to cast blame. "She wasn't ignoring her Hippocratic oath. There was a fifty-fifty chance, either way. I could go back and everything would be great, and I'd pick up where I left off in my career, no problem." Which was what Cade had hoped with all his heart would happen. "Or I could return and it would end up being too soon and the stress of playing would cause me to exacerbate my previous injury."

"Which is what happened in the end."

"Unfortunately, yeah. The thing is, there was no way to know with any certainty. Unless I did go back."

Shifting closer to him, Allison cupped both her hands around his palm. She looked into his eyes. "Was the team pressuring you?"

Cade exhaled. "Let's just say I knew what they wanted," he admitted acerbically.

For a moment, she was silent, thinking. "What would have happened had you not gone to see that particular doctor?"

Cade grimaced. "I would have had to abide by the team doctors and wait until the healing was further along. The season would have been over…which meant I would have missed my chance to pitch in the playoffs." He blew out a breath. "And with one of the other Wranglers pitchers out, too, they really needed me in the rotation. So I did what I wanted to do anyway, which was play, and I stepped up."

"And got hurt again in your third game back."

Cade nodded, remembering the moment when he'd felt his rotator cuff give out. The searing pain that had made him first double over, then sink to the ground. The loud collective gasp and then the utter heartrending silence of the crowd.

"I saw it on TV," she admitted, tearing up as she recalled. "Not during the game. But after...on the news...in replays."

"Yeah." He had to grit his teeth at the memory. "It was pretty damn awful."

"Did you know at the time how bad it was? Or did you have to wait to get to the ER to find out?"

He thought about the way he had silently cussed himself out in the ambulance, over and over again. The regret had been deeper and more devastating than the physical pain. "I didn't have to hear the doctors say it. I knew I was never going to be able to throw at the same level again."

Allison fell silent, her fingers tightening consolingly over his. Then, to his surprise, she leaned into his side, the way she always had when they were a couple.

"So you quit." She let out a long sigh and rested her head on his uninjured shoulder.

Cade figured if he was going to be honest, he might as well tell her everything. "More like I was shown the door."

She turned to better see his face, her bent knee nudging his thigh. "Just like that?" She looked horrified. "After eight years with the team?"

He knew she wanted him to tell her everyone had been there to comfort him. That his teammates had been as devastated as his family. And yeah, the other players had all been sorry for him, briefly, but they had to focus on their own performance and move on. Just as he had done when others had left the Wranglers in the past.

"It's the way professional sports works."

"They just cut you free without trying to make something work?"

Cade scoffed. "Like a front-office job or something in marketing?"

"Or I don't know." She gestured inanely. "Assistant field manager or something."

He reached for his coffee. It had gotten cold. He drank it anyway. "A position given out of pity would have only made me more miserable." Able to see she still didn't understand, he said gruffly, "Look, you can either do what they need you to do or you can't. And if you can't, you pack your bags and go. That's the way it is and always has been."

"I'm sorry."

Me, too, Cade thought. But there was no going

back, no asking for a do-over for that part of his life, anyway. In other arenas, he might have a chance to make things right. Like right here, right now. With her. At least that was what the most idealistic part of him hoped. "I would have had to move on eventually," he told her practically, "so…I'm moving on."

Funny, she didn't look as unhappy as he had figured she would, given the loss of his career and everything that went with it. The fame, the money…

Allison nodded her understanding. Pushed on. "So how is your shoulder now?" she asked gently. "Is the ice helping?"

He liked her fussing over him. Just as he liked fussing over *her*. He winked. "You tell me." He moved the bag and put her hand where the ice had been.

As her palm flattened over the bunched muscles in his chest, a mischievous twinkle appeared in her eyes. "I can see you're recovering," she said dryly. Still, she left her palm where it was. "Enough to drive home?"

That was the last place he wanted to be. Wishing he didn't want to haul her close and make love to her quite so badly, he coaxed her with a smile. "You don't want to hang out a little while longer?"

For a moment, he thought she might say yes. Then she pulled herself together and shook her head, dispelling the flirtatious mood between them. "We're going to have the kids 24/7 for the next two days," she told him soberly. "Which means tomorrow is going to be a *very* long day."

But a good one, if they were together. He let his glance linger on her softly parted lips. "Still want my help?"

"If you're up to it?" She smiled. "Yes, Cade, I do. In the meantime—" she looked around "—let's find your other shirt."

"I think it's still in the kitchen." He ripped off the tape while she went to look. When she returned, the makeshift ice pack was off.

He stood.

Instead of just handing the thermal tee over, she opened up the neck with her hands and motioned for him to bend toward her. He did, and she eased it over his head and neck, which enabled him to put his good arm through the sleeve. Then, with her assistance, he got the other arm through, too. After she helped him get the flannel shirt on over that, her eyes darkened with feminine concern. "Can you button it? We don't want you getting too cold outside."

It would have been irritating as hell to have anyone else fussing over him this way. But not Allison. When she hovered over him, it felt surprisingly good and right.

Figuring it was time for him to assert his masculinity again, he wrapped his arms around her waist and teased, "Well, we wouldn't want that."

She gazed up and blushed prettily when he pulled

her against him. She smelled like vanilla and the spicy cookies they had been baking. "I'm serious, Cade," she protested.

He knew she was.

Which was what made it easy to lower his head and kiss her. Gently at first, then with growing ardor. With a soft, low moan of surrender, she returned his embrace, just as he'd hoped, wreathing her arms about his neck and pressing the soft lusciousness of her breasts against his chest. The ridge of his desire grew, reminding them both where passion like theirs always led. That seemed to serve as some kind of wake-up call. Schooling her not to simply slide back into his life and pick up where they'd left off. She shuddered and moaned again, and then tore her lips from his.

Breathlessly, she stepped back to glare at him. "Darn it, Cade! You've got to stop acting like we are on some sort of extended date…"

That was her metaphor, not his.

Grinning at all she hadn't said, he let her show him the front door, then drawled merrily, "So, I'll see you-all tomorrow morning, then?"

Still looking deliciously disheveled, she nodded. And he walked out.

Chapter Seven

The next morning, Cade stared at Allison from the other side of the portal. Nine in the morning and she was still in a pair of ice-blue satin pajamas and what looked like a thigh-length cashmere sleep sweater now stained with something wet and brown and icky-looking. In the distance, he could hear yelling and crying, and was that something being thrown? "What happened?"

Zeus nudged Cade's thigh, then tossed his head in the direction he wanted Cade to go, while Allison ushered him inside. The fragrance of freshly made waffles and maple syrup woke his senses. "Everyone got up on the wrong side of the bed," she said, looking even more harried as the noise from the back of the house escalated exponentially.

Leaving him to follow, she ran in the direction of the melee. "Girls!" she shouted. "Come on now! Calm down!"

"She stole my breakfast!" Sienna yelled, pointing at Hazel, who was dangling the plate just out of reach.

"It's a joke!" Hazel declared.

"It's not funny!" Amber said, leaving her untouched meal and getting down on the floor to wrap her arms around Zeus's neck.

"Stop fighting. You're hurting my ears." Jade stood on tiptoes to reach the platter in the middle of the kitchen island. With a swipe of her arm, she brought it toward her so quickly it almost tumbled off the edge to join the overturned plastic orange juice bottle dripping liquid onto the floor. "I'll fix you another one."

"I don't want that," Sienna said with a pout. She pointed at the waffle already smeared with butter, powdered sugar and maple syrup, which Hazel was still holding hostage. "I want that one!"

"And you shall have it." Cade swooped in to rescue Sienna's breakfast. He set it on the place mat in front of her. Only to have her scowl and push it away.

"Well, now I don't want it," she whined.

Understandably, Allison looked as if she were about to lose her mind. He understood. He'd only been here two minutes and he was ready for the loony bin, too. His heart going out to Allison, he asked, "When did you-all wake up?"

She slid onto a stool and buried her face in her hands. "Four hours ago," she admitted miserably.

He knew how she liked things to be perfect. This was far from that. "Five a.m.?"

She nodded and peered up at him through her spread fingers. "This is our second breakfast."

"The first was cereal and milk!" Jade offered helpfully.

Allison straightened and drew in a deep breath that lifted the soft swell of her breasts. His body tightened in response, but he forced himself to concentrate on the matter at hand.

"They were hungry and I thought it might be better to have something hot this time," she explained. "Although they wanted the cold cereal earlier."

"When are Mommy and Daddy going to FaceTime us?" Sienna asked. "You said they would!"

Which maybe explained the little girl's bad behavior, Cade thought. She feared it wasn't going to happen. Again.

Allison got a roll of paper towels. He held out his hand for a few, and together, they got down to mop up the spilled juice. "Your parents should be calling us anytime now," Allison said. "At least I hope so." With a sigh, she looked at Cade. "I tried to explain the time difference between here and Switzerland."

He offered his hand and, loving the soft, delicate feel of her palm clasped in his, helped her to her feet.

"When they're having breakfast, we're having dinner," Hazel said.

"No! When we're having breakfast, they're having dinner," Amber corrected, still hugging Zeus like a lifeline to sanity.

Hazel stuck out her tongue. Sienna elbowed her. Jade pushed them both.

"In the meantime," Cade said, physically stepping in to stop another melee, "I think we should all sit down and enjoy the wonderful second breakfast Allison made while we wait to talk with your mommy and daddy." He guided each of the girls into a chair at the breakfast table.

"What if they don't call us?" Amber's lower lip quivered.

"They will," he promised. Even if he had to do the dialing himself.

Allison handed Cade a plate and silverware. She let out a quiet sigh. "Coffee?"

He wished he could hold her close, smooth the tousled hair away from her face and plant a tender kiss on her temple. Anything to soothe her and make her feel better. But they had an audience, so...best to keep it a lot more casual. He smiled. "Please."

"Plain?"

He wasn't surprised she remembered—she'd always been good at the details—but he liked it that she had. "You got it."

The moment drew out and they exchanged grown-up we're-in-this-together smiles.

Noticing, the girls squinted at them. "So what else is on your minds?" Cade asked, able to see from their petulant scowls they had other complaints.

Sienna kicked the leg of the table. "It's not fair Mommy and Daddy aren't here to take us to see Santa 'cause all our friends from school are getting to do stuff like that today."

Cade took a bite of waffle. The girls didn't know what they were missing thus far. It was melt-in-your-mouth delicious.

He gave Allison an inquiring look. She seemed to be thinking what he was: they would likely go stir-crazy if they remained in the house all day today. "We can do that with you," he said. "As soon as we find out where he is."

Allison looked at her phone. "It looks like he is going to be at the San Angelo mall today."

The girls exchanged excited grins. "Can we go?" Amber asked.

Again, Cade and Allison were of the same mind. "Absolutely," they said.

It took another twenty minutes for everyone to finish eating, and then the girls went upstairs to brush their teeth and get dressed while Cade and

Allison handled the dishes. "Any idea why Sara-beth and Shawn haven't called?" he said, now that the girls were out of earshot.

"No. I texted them both a reminder and got noth-ing."

Cade frowned. "Maybe they're just busy."

"Maybe. Would you mind finishing up here so I can go up and help the girls with their hair and get dressed, too?"

"Take your time."

Thanks to a quadruplet wardrobe crisis, it was another forty-five minutes before all five females were ready to leave the house. But in his view, it had been worth the wait. The girls all looked cute in holiday sweaters and jeans. And Allison looked absolutely incredible. She smelled like the jasmine-scented shampoo and soap she favored. Her dark hair was a soft, silky cloud about her face and shoulders. Snug-fitting jeans cloaked her fine derriere and legs. The dark green turtleneck sweater brought out the pine green of her long-lashed eyes. And finally, a subtle application of color enhanced the soft lush-ness of her lips. "Sorry about the wait." She patted his arm as she passed.

"Worth it," he murmured back. *So worth it...* She tossed him a wry look.

A few moments later, they gathered up everyone's coats and put them on, and headed out to Sarabeth's Suburban.

"What happens if Mommy and Daddy call when we aren't home?" Jade asked worriedly.

Allison opened the passenger door. "I have my cell phone with me, remember?" She helped the girls climb in. "And Cade has his, too. So they will be able to reach us."

The girls relaxed. Allison turned on Christmas music, and the thirty-minute drive to the neighboring city was filled with lots of music and exuberant singing.

The girls grew even more excited as they made their way past the stores to the North Pole village set up in the sunny mall atrium. Elves and Mrs. Claus greeted all the newcomers while parents and children stood in line.

Fortunately, because it was still early, the lines weren't too long. "Take a picture and text it to Mommy and Daddy!" Jade said.

"Good idea." Cade lined up the girls with their backs to the village and their arms around each other. "Say 'cheese'!" The girls giggled. He got the shot.

"And one with Allison, too!" he directed, unable to help but think what a wonderful mother she would make. If only she had still wanted to have kids, that was. Instead, as far as she'd let on, she was now dedicated to remaining single and unencumbered...

"Want us to take your picture?" Allison asked.

Cade noted a fortysomething man with a goatee,

in a Wranglers MLB cap and flannel shirt and jeans, standing in front of a home goods shop.

He had a woman around the same age and in similar attire next to him. They were both staring at him. Watching him and Allison and the kids in a way that was making Cade uncomfortable.

Hoping it wasn't a disgruntled fan—there were plenty of them since he had pitched the final losing game in the last playoffs—he turned away. That part of his life was over now. It was going to stay over. "Nah. Let's take some pictures of Santa and Mrs. Claus and the elves instead…"

The quadruplets cooperated. Soon, it was their turn to talk to Santa. They climbed onto Saint Nick's lap, two at a time, and whispered what they wanted for Christmas in his ear.

He told them all he would do his best.

Finished, they headed out of the village "gate" and stood next to Cade. Out of the corner of his eye, he saw the man in the Wranglers MLB cap still staring unhappily at Cade and looking as if he might approach. Determined not to let that happen, he said, "Who wants ice cream?"

Allison blinked. "Before lunch?"

He winked, gathering up the girls. "After brunch…"

"Everything okay?" she asked, as they headed for the food court.

Cade didn't want to turn around to check. He would head the guy off if necessary, give him a chance to say his piece, but first he wanted to get Allison and the girls settled. "Yeah."

They found a table. Cade took the orders and then headed off to get the treats while Allison stayed behind with the girls. As he'd expected, the man in the ball cap slipped into line behind him. "Lockhart."

Here we go...

Cade turned with the polite grin he reserved for meeting strangers. "How are you?"

"Not good, after the way you blew the playoffs for the Wranglers."

Out of the corner of his eye, Cade saw the woman taking photos...and maybe a video...with her phone. Great. Just what he needed. To be back on social media.

Not about to give them anything of interest, Cade kept a poker face. "I take it you really wanted to see them make it all the way to the World Series this year?"

"Damn right I did, and so did all the other fans."

Cade nodded. "I think everyone was disappointed."

"It was your fault," the man insisted, beginning to get a little belligerent.

Cade saw Allison looking alarmed. Luckily, the girls hadn't noticed yet.

A mall policeman had, however, and he approached the man in the cap. "Sir? I'd like to speak to you about your vehicle."

The angry fan started. "What?"

"I think there is a problem," the cop continued. "If you'll just come with me, I'll explain..."

Cade sent the officer a silent look of thanks, then headed back to the table. "They're out of the kind we want. So how about we all go to the Dairy Barn back in Laramie?"

Because it was lunchtime by the time they arrived, they ended up getting the girls hot dogs, fries and ice cream. When they had finished eating, because it had turned out to be a sunny day, with the temperatures hovering in the low sixties, they headed over to the park. While the girls played on the playground, Cade and Allison watched from a nearby bench. She lifted her chin and locked eyes with him. "You want to tell me what happened back at the mall?"

Briefly, Cade explained.

"You know the woman with him was taking pictures of the confrontation."

He sighed. "Yeah, I saw."

She turned toward him, her bent knee rubbing against his. Her soft lips twisted into a frown. "Does that happen often?"

He draped his arm along the back of the bench. "Never in Laramie County. Not often in San Angelo. In Dallas…a lot, actually. Although there, I had as many folks telling me that they loved me as I had people telling me they hated the way I played. And then a certain percentage were just starstruck and wanted an autograph or selfie."

She released a breath and held his gaze with the

kindness and compassion he had come to expect from her. "Is that why you moved back home?" she asked softly.

Aware he wanted her to be his again, more than ever, he shrugged, looked her in the eye and said, "I moved here because I wanted to have a regular non-celebrity life. Settle down. Get married. And have a family."

Cade was so sincere and matter-of-fact, Allison felt her jaw drop. "Do the local ladies know that?" she asked.

Inscrutable emotion came and went in his espresso eyes. "How would I know?"

She'd always wondered if she had made a mistake, calling it quits with him when she had. Instead of waiting around to see if they could make it work while he got used to life in the big time. But she hadn't and now there was no way to know what might have happened. "Have you told anyone this?" she demanded, still feeling a little stunned by his declaration. "Like your family, who wouldn't hesitate to put out the word…?"

His smile deepened, his voice turning gruffly sexy. "I told *you*."

There had been a time, back when they'd been dating, when she would have given anything to have him say that to her, but that was then, when she'd still had a romantic bone left in her body.

Now all she wanted was the kind of lifelong security that came from not depending on anyone but yourself.

"Miss Allison! Mr. Cade! Look at us!" the girls shouted from atop the climbing fort.

Relieved by the distraction, Allison waved while Cade called his encouragement.

Her phone chimed, signaling an incoming message. "Finally," she said, thinking it was a text from Sarabeth and Shawn. Instead, it was an email from Laurel Grimes at HITN.

"Everything okay?" Cade asked.

"The latest challenge. I have to get two holiday trees and decorate them, one for a family, another for myself—as a single woman. Then, by nine a.m. Monday morning, I need to make a short video and write an accompanying blog post, detailing how to do this all yourself."

"Doesn't sound that hard for someone with your talent," he praised.

Allison huffed. "Says someone who has never had to design anything while simultaneously babysitting quadruplets all weekend!"

Cade wrapped his arm around her shoulders and tugged her in close to his side. "Good thing you've got me, then, isn't it?"

Going to the tree lot and picking out two seven-and-a-half-foot trees while simultaneously keeping watch over the quadruplets took up the remainder of the afternoon.

"Can we get mistletoe?" Jade asked, as they headed for the checkout stand, Cade carrying one tree and a lot worker the other.

"Mistletoe?" he repeated, as if he couldn't possibly have heard right.

What did they know about mistletoe? Allison wondered.

"It makes grown-ups happy," Amber explained.

"We want our mommy and daddy to be happy when they get back from Switzerland," Sienna added.

Cade shot Allison a mischievous glance that warmed her from head to toe. "Then mistletoe it is," he declared, picking up a beribboned strand and placing that on the counter, too.

The girls giggled with excitement. Amber clapped her hands with delight while Hazel smacked her lips together and made loud kissing sounds, which in turn made everyone around them chuckle and look speculatively at Cade and Allison. Which, consequently, made Allison recall with disturbing clarity exactly how much fun it was to kiss Cade and be kissed by him in return. Even without the time-honored holiday tradition!

The girls got even sillier on the ride home, yet were yawning when they finally entered their house. "Can we watch TV?" they asked.

"Don't you want to help put up the tree?" Allison asked, surprised at their quickly dwindling interest.

More yawns. "We're tired." Jade already had her lovey blanket.

The other girls were quick to follow suit. "Please, Miss Allison," Amber said.

Hazel and Sienna climbed onto the couch, waiting. They looked so bone-tired Allison's heart went out to them. It had been a very long day. "All right, how about half an hour," she said.

The girls nodded.

When she had their favorite TV show going, Cade came back in with Zeus. "Next question," he said, inclining his head toward the roof of Sarabeth's Suburban, still sitting in the driveway. "Where are you going to put these trees up?"

"One will go to my place. The other should probably be put up here."

"You want to do it now?"

"While the girls are well occupied? Sure. Makes sense."

They walked out together. Both trees had been secured to the luggage rack on the top of the vehicle. He held the tree in place while she cut the heavy twine. Beginning to realize what a good team they still made, Allison murmured, "I just hope Sarabeth and Shawn won't mind us putting a Christmas tree in their formal living room while they are gone."

Cade's broad shoulders and strong arms flexed as

he lifted the pine tree down and set it on the ground. "You could ask them, if they'd ever answer our calls and texts."

"I know, right?" Allison paused to get the metal tree stand that had come with the purchase of the tree. "They must be really busy over there." At least she hoped that was all it was.

When he flashed her a curious look, she pushed on. "But I guess if they do, we can always un-decorate this one or get another for them to put up in a different room in their traditional way."

He waited for her to open the front door and hold it in place. "Seems like a lot of unnecessary trouble, but…yeah…I guess you could all do that."

The tree was so thick and full he barely avoided running into her as he brushed by. She set up the stand where she wanted it in front of the picture window, then knelt down to screw the tree trunk in place.

Cade held out a hand, and his warm, strong fingers covered hers. Their eyes locked and held as he helped her up, and she felt a tingling moment of awareness. One that hinted resistance to the stunning chemistry between them might be futile after all. More unsettling, he seemed equally smitten… Chivalrously, he released his grip on her hand. "Where are you going to get the family tree decorations?" he asked.

Trying not to think how very much she wanted to kiss and hold him again, never mind what a fun, family-oriented day they'd had, Allison waved an airy hand. Just because she and Cade felt very much like a couple now did not mean it would continue once their babysitting gig ended. She needed to remember that. "Oh, I've got tons of decorations stored in boxes in my garage since I do a different theme and design every year."

The corners of his lips twitched with mirth.

She put a little more distance between them. Propped her hands indignantly on her hips. Chiding drolly back, "What?"

Eyes twinkling, he slid a hand underneath his rough-hewn jaw. "I was just thinking about the trees both our families had, back when we were dating."

She warmed at the sentiment in his low voice. "With all the random kiddie-made ornaments."

Coming nearer, he quirked a brow and continued with comically exaggerated seriousness. "They were definitely one of a kind."

How was it he always smelled so good? Like rain-drenched cedar and brisk winter air? How was it he always made her want him so much? Even when she knew he still had the power to break her heart. Noting she had gotten a little tree sap on her hands, and barely had escaped getting it on her clothing, Allison ducked into the bathroom tucked beneath the stairs. "Yes, well, I think the ones I do for the network are going to have to be a lot more sophisticated than those were."

He joined her at the sink and washed his hands, too. "Sophisticated isn't everything."

Trying not to notice how small the space suddenly felt, Allison turned to face him, her hip bumping up against his. "You didn't think that way eight years ago."

Cade tossed her a contrite look and retorted gruffly, "Eight years ago I was a fool." He bent down and captured her lips with his. "No more…"

She trembled as a lightning bolt of desire shot through her. He took her in his arms and cradled her masterfully against his chest. The kiss that followed was everything she desired—lush and evocative, sweet and searching. And oh so deliciously tempting. Her spirits soared. Her knees went weak, her lips opened to the dizzying pressure of his, and once again making out with him felt like the most intimate thing they could ever do.

Aware she was very close to letting down the rest of her defenses and falling for him all over again, Allison pushed on his chest. Calling on every ounce of self-control she had, she broke off the kiss and stepped back, her emotions in turmoil.

She wanted him. That was clear.

She didn't want to be hurt by him again.

"I don't know what I'm going to do with you," she murmured in exasperation, as her heart continued to race. He hadn't pursued her this avidly or thrilled her so much when they were actually dating!

"I don't know," he drawled in return, rubbing his lips across the back of her knuckles. Once again, he searched her eyes. "Maybe kiss me some more right now? Or better yet," he queried even more softly and tenderly, "give me a second chance?"

Chapter Eight

His heart in his throat, Cade waited for Allison to respond.

"Second chance," she repeated, as if that were the last thing in the world she wanted. "Cade, if we were going to make this work, we would have done so during the eight years we were together!"

He studied her set lips, forcing himself to tamp down the urge to haul her into his arms and kiss her even more thoroughly this time. "We're older now. Wiser."

She couldn't debate that. But it didn't mean she agreed with what he thought they should do next. "I…"

Her phone chimed to signal an incoming text. "Saved by the bell?" he teased.

With a rueful smile, she gave him another long, telling look, then pulled her phone from her pocket. "It's Sarabeth. She says, and I quote, 'There is so much going on now. Can't talk. But I will definitely call tomorrow.'"

"Oh, boy," Cade said.

"The girls aren't going to like this," Allison murmured in concern.

"No joke."

Allison briefly typed in the outgoing text line: Okay, but please call then. They miss you terribly! She showed Cade. "What do you think?"

"Good. They need to know they aren't doing all they should."

Allison sent the text. Then put her phone in the back pocket of her jeans, drawing Cade's attention to her slender hips. A mixture of worry and reluctance lit her pretty eyes. "Well, I guess we better tell them."

He nodded.

The girls were right where they'd left them, snuggled up together, watching the end of their TV show. "Girls, we have some news," Allison said. She went on to tell them what Sarabeth had texted.

Cade had half expected an outbreak of hysteria. Instead, the girls simply yawned and nodded. "Is it dinnertime yet?" Amber asked.

"I want grilled cheese," Jade said, stretching.

"And clementine oranges." Sienna climbed down off the sofa.

"Plus, carrot sticks and ranch dressing." Hazel stood on her head, her back against the sofa cushions, her feet up in the air. Briefly, she tried to bicycle, but she was off balance and the pedaling motion of her legs turned into a somersault onto the floor.

Allison smiled at all four girls, then Cade. "I think we can handle that," she said.

There she went, Cade thought with satisfaction. Saying *we* instead of *I* again. Maybe they weren't so far away from being a couple again as she wanted to think.

Glad for the task at hand, and the interruption that had saved her from having to talk more with Cade about the possibility of them giving their relationship another go, Allison enlisted everyone's help. She put the sandwiches together and cut carrots into sticks while Cade manned the grill. The girls set the table and peeled the clementines.

When they sat down together, talk turned to the various events of the day. "I don't think you ever told us what you asked Santa to bring you," Allison said, hoping to keep the evening pleasantly Christmassy.

Jade answered first. "I asked him to bring my mommy and daddy stuff to make them both happy."

Amber used her fingertip to smear ranch dressing all over her carrot stick. "I asked Santa to bring Daddy another cell phone so he could call Mommy twice as much when he is away."

That didn't quite make sense. But okay...

Hazel grinned. "I asked Santa to bring lots of mistletoe to make them kiss again."

Across the table, Cade sent Allison an ornery look. Insides tingling, she tried not to overtly react.

"But we got some at the tree lot," Sienna protested, as Allison focused on the girls instead of the memory of Cade's hot, soulful kisses once more.

"We can have more mistletoe," Amber added, practical as ever.

"Yeah, we could put it everywhere in the house!" Hazel said.

That would be a land mine and a half, given how prone Cade suddenly was to putting the moves on her. On the other hand, when Sarabeth and Shawn returned, lots of excuses for kissing might be just what they needed... "What about you, Sienna?" Allison asked. "What did you ask Santa for?"

Sienna sobered. "A magic wand so I could wave it and make Mommy and Daddy fall in love again."

Wow, Allison thought, her heart going out to all four of them. She and Cade exchanged looks.

"Those are very generous gifts," he noted kindly, steadfastly ignoring the troubling implications beneath.

"But didn't you ask Santa for anything for yourselves?" Allison pressed. Knowing if they had, she needed to pass the information along to Sarabeth and Shawn.

For a moment, the girls looked perplexed.

They exchanged glances that were suddenly wise beyond their years. "We want Mommy and Daddy to be happy again," Sienna concluded finally.

"How do you know that they're not?" Allison asked quietly.

Shrugs all around.

Hazel drank her milk. "Because they don't talk or laugh or have fun."

"They're just really quiet." Amber ate her sandwich.

"And not good quiet," Jade added with a concerned frown. "Time-out quiet."

Cade nodded to indicate he was listening. Allison did the same.

The confessions had been cathartic. But neither she nor Cade had any solutions. Those would have to come from Shawn and Sarabeth when they returned to the States.

"Well," Cade said finally, changing the subject with sudden attention-grabbing drama. "I'm hurt. Nobody even asked! Does anyone want to know what *I* would like Santa to bring *me* for Christmas?"

Finally, a challenge the girls could meet! "A new bicycle!" Amber guessed, excited. "One that doesn't have training wheels!"

"I think he wants a new doll baby." Hazel grinned, back to being as deliberately silly as usual. "Hey—"

she spread her hands wide "—boys can play with dolls, too."

Cade's laughter was rich and masculine. "That's right. In fact—" he leaned across the table confidingly "—I spent a lot of time playing with dolls when I was your age. And you know why? Because I played with my younger sisters and that's what they wanted to do!"

The girls giggled at the notion of big, strong masculine Cade cradling a pretend baby.

"Jade, what do you think Santa should bring Cade?" Allison asked.

"An art easel. One with a tray that will hold all your crayons and markers!" Jade beamed.

"And Sienna?" Cade prompted.

Sienna contemplated. "I think Santa should bring you a very long jump rope. So everyone can skip rope with you."

"Hmm." Cade stroked the evening stubble on his chin. "Very good idea."

"And maybe some mistletoe for your house, too," Hazel joked mischievously. "So you can get lots and lots of kisses, too!"

"Well, I think we know what the girls all want Santa to bring them for Christmas," Allison said an hour and a half later.

The quadruplets were asleep. Cade had returned with Zeus from the pet's evening walk. He looked exceptionally appealing with hair windblown, his handsome face ruddy from the cold.

"A little obvious, hmm, in their suggested gifts for me?" He unsnapped the leash. Zeus looked up at Cade adoringly, which earned him a pat on the head. Then he ambled into the kitchen to get some water.

Time with the quadruplets was always so jam-packed with activity. She reveled in the quiet time with Cade after the girls were in bed. "I already texted Sarabeth about the doll, jump rope, easel and bike."

He sent her a mischievous glance. "Nothing about the mistletoe?"

The memory of Cade's interactions with the girls generated a wave of warmth. He was so kind and understanding, yet funny, and not afraid to set boundaries with them, too. All in all, the perfect dad. If only the two of them had married and had a child together! How wonderful would that have been? But they hadn't stayed together, so… Allison swallowed and forced herself to come back to earth. "I think that's supposed to be a surprise when they come home from Switzerland."

He sauntered closer, lingering nearby while she reviewed the long to-do list she had been working on.

Cade gave her the lazy once-over. "I meant the mistletoe for my house," he drawled. "I noticed you didn't weigh in."

She wished she were immune to the devilry in his

espresso eyes. She wished she could let down her guard and let him take care of her. It was Christmas, after all. But their life was complicated enough at the moment. She needed to be careful what she risked. "I don't think you need any help in that arena," she said dryly, pushing past him, detailed list still in hand. "I, however, do." She walked back into the formal living room. "I really need to get the lights on the family tree this evening, if I'm going to make the Monday deadline HITN gave me."

Reminded of her goal, he was all business once again. "Want me to help?"

Maybe this was what they needed. Time together that was all work and no play. With no opportunity to veer off track. "Sure." She opened up one of the storage boxes she had brought over earlier. "If you don't mind being precise."

His dark brows furrowed. "What precision is required stringing lights on a tree?"

Allison got out the seamstress tape. "I measure."

He blinked. "The tree?"

"The distance from each branch and each visible bulb."

Looking stymied, he narrowed his gaze. "You're kidding. Wait. You're *not* kidding?"

She shrugged, her eyes sparkling. "Hey, if it's too much for you…" she teased.

He squared his broad shoulders. "I think I'm man enough to handle it."

"We'll see." Allison moved the step stool closer to the tree. Cade held the lights while she started winding the strand around the top branches. For a few minutes, they worked in silence, but it quickly became clear that physically, anyway, they were as in sync with each other as they always had been, and not much direction was needed. Which made her wonder, in turn, if they would still be that way in bed...

Not that she should be thinking about *that*, when there were other things they needed to discuss while they had a chance.

She checked her strands for placement, found them as precise as she'd hoped. Then started to step down from the stool. "What do you think about the other stuff the girls said?"

Cade cupped her elbow, to steady her, his touch gentle but firm. "You mean the gifts they wanted for their parents?"

No longer at eye level with him, Allison looked up. She searched his expression. "It was a little sad, wasn't it?"

His eyes darkened. "Grown-ups always think kids don't pick up on things," he said in a low, brooding tone, "but they do."

They went back to stringing lights. "You didn't seem all that surprised by what their requests to Santa revealed," Allison noted.

"Shawn told me he was hoping the trip abroad

would be good for him and Sarabeth. They haven't had any time for just the two of them since the quadruplets were born."

Allison found herself taking her best friend's side. "It's kind of hard, especially with him traveling all the time for work."

"But it's hard for him, too, when he thinks she is doing everything possible to avoid being alone with him whenever he is around."

Allison halted, shocked. She turned to face Cade, her shoulder nudging his chest. "Shawn said that?"

He remained where he was, looking down at her. "Not in so many words, but…I think that's the gist of it."

Alarm sent a shiver through her body. Momentarily forgetting her task, Allison turned so she was facing Cade directly. "Is he ready to throw in the towel on their marriage?"

Cade did a double take. "Far from it. Why would you think that?"

"Because Sarabeth told me that she was afraid the real reason Shawn was so insistent she go with him to the annual retreat for his tech company was because he was going to tell her he didn't love her anymore and he wanted a divorce!"

"Whoa. Talk about being on the wrong page!" Cade said.

"For both of them."

Silence fell between them as they finished stringing the lights on the bottom branches.

"Think we should straighten out the misunderstanding?" Allison asked eventually. She stepped back to admire their handiwork. All seemed as perfect as she had planned.

Cade sighed. In a low, gruff voice, he predicted, "Hopefully, they're already talking things out, which is why they haven't called the girls."

"Or...they aren't talking at all," Allison worried out loud. Feeling unbearably thirsty, she went into the kitchen and opened the fridge. She got out the pitcher of filtered water. "And they're both really miserable and they don't want the girls to pick up on it."

Cade got out two glasses and held them while she poured. "Sure you're giving them enough credit? The two of them started dating in high school."

And, unlike us, Allison thought, *they never split up*.

"They're still together now. Sixteen years as a couple is something to be proud of. They may have hit a rough patch—" Cade clinked glasses with her, sipped "—but I believe they'll work it out."

"Wow." Allison drained her glass, then set it down on the counter. "You're really a lot more romantic than I ever knew."

Cade set his glass down, too. "Well, then that's my bad." He caught her around the waist and danced her over to the archway between the living room and the formal dining room.

"What are you doing?" she asked, laughing.

Mischief glimmered in his eyes. "Look up."

She did, her mouth dropping open in surprise. "When did you hang the mistletoe?"

He flashed her a crooked grin. "When you were helping the girls get their showers." He tunneled his hands through her hair and tilted her face up to his. "Of course, we have to try it out properly to see if it works…"

"Cade," she chided, a thrill soaring through her. "Not another kiss."

His lips touched hers. "Yes, another kiss…"

The next thing she knew, their lips were fused. Instinct took over and she was all the way against him, wrapped in his strong, steady warmth. His kiss was romantic, sweet and tender. A bridge to their past, their present and maybe, Allison thought wistfully, even their future… Luxuriating in the scent and feel of him, so brisk and masculine and familiar, she rose on tiptoe, returning the caress, letting herself feel everything he wanted her to feel. Until he finally lifted his head. "Well? What do you think?" he teased. "Potent enough?"

Aware she had been caught in a trap of her own making, Allison groaned. "You are impossible, Cade Lockhart."

"Determined." He brought her in for a close, comforting hug, then whispered in her ear, "And you know how I am when I want something…"

She did. She also knew how she was when *she* wanted something. Forcing herself to put on the brakes and come to her senses, she splayed her hand across his chest. "Which is why you have to go home right now."

Chapter Nine

"Remarkably calm here this morning," Cade remarked, as he walked in some ten hours later, Zeus by his side. He was wearing a black North Face jacket, dark-rinse jeans and a charcoal-gray thermal knit shirt. He hadn't bothered to shave, but his dark hair was agreeably rumpled and shiny clean. He smelled like cedarwood-scented soap and shampoo. And the cool-mint toothpaste he favored. Just looking at him made her want to tempt fate and kiss him again. Which wasn't surprising, given the fact she'd dreamed about him all night.

"Where are the little ones?" he asked, looking around.

"In the kitchen, eating their breakfast," she returned very quietly. Then gave him a look, one temporary parental figure to another. "And let's not jinx it."

His shoulders flexed as he shrugged out of his coat and hung it over the newel post next to Zeus's leash. "It's you I should be worried about, then?" he teased, his gaze raking over her, lighting little fires of awareness everywhere it touched.

Only in the sense that I might do something really foolish and fall for you all over again. She tossed her hair triumphantly. "No. I'll have you know I got up at five o'clock this morning, so I'd have plenty of time to shower and get ready for the day and drink a cup of coffee before the girls woke up." It had helped her immensely to have that quiet time alone, to pull herself together and plan everything from what she was going to feed the girls to how she was going to keep Cade at arm's length, emotionally.

"Good for you." He strode toward her, looking relaxed and capable. "Zeus and I were up, too. We took a walk and then went back to the house, where he ate breakfast and then went back to bed and slept until I got back from my morning run."

It was easy to imagine them doing just that. But then, Cade always had been an early riser. Bounding out of bed in the mornings with a ton of energy and a cheerful attitude.

Sienna ran out to join them. "Mr. Cade is here!" she shouted over her shoulder.

"And Zeus?" Amber asked, running out, too. Catching sight of the family pet, she grinned and dropped down to wreathe her arms about his neck. She buried her face in his black-and-white muzzle. "Oh, my sweet doggy," she murmured happily, "I missed you so much."

"I did, too." Hazel joined in the hugs, then dropped down to lie on the floor and prop her hips and legs in the air. She pedaled madly. "Look at me, everyone! I'm riding a bicycle!"

"Wow!" Cade said.

Not to be outdone, Jade grabbed his hand. "Come see the drawings I did!"

Hazel, Amber and Sienna tagged along. Together, they made their way back to the kitchen. The girls returned to their breakfasts.

Not sure whether he had eaten or not, just knowing in the past he had always been hungry, probably due to the sheer number of calories he expended, Allison said, "Help yourself."

"Thanks." Cade poured cereal into a bowl, then topped it with fruit and milk.

Allison's computer tablet signaled an incoming FaceTime request from overseas. *Finally*, she thought.

"Is it Mommy and Daddy?" the girls asked.

It certainly was, Allison noted with relief. But instead of calling from a hotel room, they were phoning from what appeared to be Shawn's *hospital bedside*?

"Hey, girls." Shawn and Sarabeth greeted their children with determined good cheer. "Allison. Cade."

Sarabeth continued informatively, "We're sorry it took us so long to call you again, but Daddy had an accident skiing during a team-building exercise yesterday. He broke his leg in two places." She reached over and took his hand, squeezing it firmly. "So, he had to have surgery last night!"

No wonder they hadn't called, Allison thought, her heart going out to them.

"Does it hurt?" Amber asked.

"No. I'm good." Shawn continued to hold his wife's hand with an affection Allison hadn't seen between the couple for quite a while.

Sarabeth answered a few more questions from their daughters, then went on to explain, "Daddy has to stay in the hospital a little bit, so we won't be coming home tomorrow as originally planned."

The girls groaned in unison, suddenly looking as if they were going to cry.

"But you could do a couple of things to help us," Shawn went on cheerfully. "First, Mommy and I are going to need some help decorating the house for Christmas this year, so do you think you can help us out with that?"

"Yes!" the kids cried, getting excited again.

"And then, of course, my cast is going to need to be decorated, too!" He moved the sheet to show them the plain white exterior that extended from ankle to midthigh.

"We can help with that," Jade volunteered. Her sisters agreed.

"Great." Shawn smiled.

Sarabeth and Shawn asked more questions of the girls. They heard about baking cookies after school, the visit to the mall Santa, eating peppermint ice cream and buying not just one but two Christmas trees at the lot! One for Allison's house and one for theirs.

"Well, sounds like you-all have been *very* busy," Sarabeth praised. "But now Daddy and I have to talk to Mr. Cade and Miss Allison about some grown-up things, so how about you-all go upstairs and brush your teeth and comb your hair and make your beds?"

"Okay, Mommy!" The kids blew kisses at the screen and scampered off.

When the coast was clear, Allison and Cade sat together in front of the screen. "It's probably going to be another four or five days before the doctors will let Shawn fly home to the States," Sarabeth warned, matter-of-fact, "so can you two continue to help out or do we need to hire someone to come in and care for the girls?"

Allison and Cade exchanged glances. Relieved

to be of one mind, she squeezed his hand and said, "It's no problem."

Cade nodded and squeezed back. "We've got this."

More instructions followed. Then Sarabeth and Shawn promised to call again the next day, and they ended the FaceTime chat.

Upstairs, it sounded like things were getting a little rowdy. In a good way this time. Allison wanted to talk to Cade about the latest developments, but first… "Hang on."

She went to the bottom of the staircase. Zeus was already there, slowly making his way up. "Girls!" she called. "How's it going up there?"

Cade stood next to her. He wrapped his hand around his mouth to concentrate the sound. "What are you all doing?" he inquired, taking a more direct approach.

Loud giggles followed.

Then footsteps down the hall. "We are *definitely* not jumping on our beds," Sienna declared.

"And we're *especially* not hitting each other with our pillows!" Hazel added in faux seriousness.

Amber and Jade appeared beside them, out of breath. "We just need five more minutes," Jade said, holding up a hand.

"Zeus is keeping his eye on us," Amber added, wrapping her arm around him.

"Okay, five minutes," Allison said. "Just don't be too wild."

"O-kay!" The girls shrieked and ran off.

Cade grinned at her. Looking relaxed. Happy. And powerfully masculine. Reminding her that he filled up her heart and her soul the way no one ever had. Or ever would. "Why, Miss Allison, that was almost laid-back," he said.

She propped her hands on her hips and retorted good-naturedly, "Is that a roundabout way of calling me *prissy*, Mr. Cade?"

His grin widened. "Oh, I would never do that, Miss Allison." His eyes sparkled.

Instead, he would take her in his arms at the slightest provocation and kiss her, until she was breathlessly begging for more.

And that would be dangerous indeed.

Attempting to keep her mind on the mundane, instead of the potent chemistry sizzling between them, she marshaled her defenses and brushed by him. "Want some more coffee? I need some."

He smiled again. "Sounds good."

They stood opposite each other, in the kitchen, mugs in hand, too restless to sit while upstairs the merriment continued unabated. "They're a lot happier, now that they've spoken with their parents," he observed. "Think they'll stay that way?"

"My guess?" she responded, reminding him she was as new to this substitute-parenting stuff as he was. "Not for four to five days."

"There will be a lot of ups and downs."

"Probably." Allison sighed, getting the feel of what it would be like to lean on him again. Not that anything but a potential rekindling of their physical relationship was in the cards right now... And she still didn't know how wise that was. Mostly because she couldn't see herself surrendering her physical self to Cade without also surrendering her heart and soul. With effort, she forced her attention back to the problem they were currently facing. "Speaking of which... Did you notice Sarabeth and Shawn were holding hands?"

"I did," Cade confirmed.

"Funny, isn't it, how tragedy and/or hardship has a way of bringing people back together," Allison murmured.

And not just their married friends.

But her and Cade, too.

"I'm surprised Allison didn't come with you," Cade's mom said several hours later after he'd walked into their ranch house, the four girls in tow.

The girls spied his brother Gabe's quintuplets—who were their preschool buddies—and ran off to join the three girls and two boys at the arts-and-crafts station his mom had set up on the long oak table in the dining room. Two of Cade's sisters, the artist turned sign company owner MacKenzie, in for a few days from Fort Worth, and Jillian, a botanist who specialized in antique roses, waved at him, then went back to supervising the nine kids seated on the benches. "She had to work."

"So it's true?" Carol asked. "She is up for a big-time TV job?"

Cade nodded. "If HITN decides her brand is the way they want to go. That's not for certain yet."

His dad joined them. "But she's got a good chance?"

"Yep," Cade said, as proud and happy for her as he was worried. Because if this situation didn't work out the way Allison wanted, she would be heartbroken.

He walked into the kitchen and helped himself to some of the mulled cider warming on the stove.

"Well, that's ironic," his doctor-brother Gabe said. "You finally both come back to Laramie County and start to make amends with each other, and now she's the one who is leaving."

"She hasn't left yet," Cade said, beginning to feel a little irritated by all the poking and prodding into his love life.

His sister Faith walked in. A social worker like his mom, she and her deployed navy SEAL husband were now trying to become foster parents, too. "A friend of mine from the high school said she saw you there last week. Looked like you might be interviewing for a job."

Jeez. Was nothing private? Cade shrugged. "I was just talking to my old baseball coach."

Faith noted, "While wearing a sport coat and tie?"

He shrugged again. "I felt like getting dressed up."

"Word is Coach is retiring," Travis, the only cow-boy besides his dad in the bunch, said, helping himself to some cider, too.

"Hmm," Cade said and left it at that.

Seeing the quadruplets were well supervised for the moment, Cade looked at the wood box next to the big stone fireplace. "I'll bring some more wood in." He headed out, but to his consternation, his father followed close behind.

This was no surprise. His adoptive father had always known when he was upset. Starting when Cade had come to him as a grieving, angry foster kid. Looking back, Cade was surprised that Carol and Robert hadn't given up on him. Especially because in Cade's mind back then, there was no way the level-headed rancher could take the place of his ebullient, former minor-league-baseball-playing birth dad. Any more than he'd thought that the ever-practical and always giving Carol could take the place of his care-free pottery-making-artisan mother. But no matter how much trouble he had given them, Robert and Carol had refused to give up on him. Plus, they had understood from the outset how important it was to Cade to keep baseball, the only lasting link he had with his late father, in his life. And hence, Robert had spent hours every week pitching and throwing with Cade, long after the ranch work was done. Cade had loved the extra attention then. Now, with his life in flux, he wasn't sure he wanted it.

"I can get this, Dad," he said.

The silver at Robert's temples did nothing to slow him down. Working cattle and riding horses kept him as strong and fit as ever. "It'll go faster if there are two of us."

Cade didn't want it to go faster. He sorted through the kindling at tortoise speed. His dad squinted at him. "So what's going on, son? Are you worried you won't get the position?"

Belatedly realizing his dad might have some valuable advice to give, Cade exhaled. "Coach said there are a couple of problems."

"What happened in Dallas," Robert guessed.

Cade filled up the metal wood box. He chose his words carefully. "There is concern that if I cut a few corners and came back too soon for my own health, I might encourage players on my team to do so, too."

His dad knew that wasn't true. Cade would never jeopardize anyone else. "What else?" the older man prodded.

"My ambition. That it again might be too much."

His dad folded his arms. "What is your plan to overcome all that?"

Cade swallowed. "I don't know yet," he admitted gruffly. "I've got a few days to get back to them."

Robert clapped him on the shoulder. "I'm sure you'll think of something."

Cade hoped so, too.

Although strangely enough, it wasn't the biggest problem he had looming right now...

"What does Allison think of all this?" His dad walked with him toward the house.

Cade saw no reason not to admit, "She wants me to be happy, Dad. I want her to get what she wants, too."

His dad paused, well short of the back door. "Even if it means leaving Laramie County?"

Cade turned to face him. "That's the beauty of a cable television show. It literally can film anywhere."

The question was, where would Allison want that to be? And why did it suddenly matter to him so darn much? It wasn't like they were a couple again. Not yet, anyway...

"How are the trees going?" Laurel Grimes asked Allison over the phone at seven o'clock Sunday evening.

"Good," she fibbed, although that wasn't quite true, since neither one was entirely finished yet. Worse, she was later than promised, packing up, to go back over to Sarabeth and Shawn's to help Cade get the girls ready for bed and tucked in. Simultaneously working and babysitting was harder than she'd thought it would be.

"Jennifer Moore has already turned hers in, and I have to tell you, they're both gorgeous. The one in her loft is eighteen feet tall."

Allison rubbed at the tension in her temples. "Are you trying to discourage me?"

"No," Laurel soothed. "I just want to know you're giving it everything you've got."

"I am." The doorbell rang. She looked at the door and saw Cade through the glass windows that framed both sides of the portal. "Listen, I've got to go, but I promise I'll have everything posted before nine o'clock tomorrow morning."

Laurel Grimes paused, as if able to sense how overwhelmed Allison felt. "That's wonderful to hear, because we're counting on you."

Allison rubbed the bridge of her nose. "I know, Laurel, and I appreciate the opportunity to vie for this position. I promise I won't disappoint." She hung up as the doorbell rang again.

"Coming!" She raced to get it. Cade stood on the porch. No one on either side of him. He did, however, have a to-go bag from the Cowgirl Café in hand.

Her joy at seeing him was tempered by concern. "Where are the girls?"

He was quick to reassure her. "At their house. Being babysat by my sisters Jillian, Faith and Mac-Kenzie. I thought you might need some help."

More like the kind of emotional support only he could give. She bit her lip, ushering him in. "I do. And I don't."

He slanted her a glance. "What does that mean?"

Suddenly feeling unutterably fragile, she sighed,

once again aware how cozy and domestic this all felt. "It means yes, I could use your help, if you were an interior designer. But—" she drew a bolstering breath "—I am supposed to be doing this the way a single woman likely would, which is all by herself." And not with the help of one very sexy, very attentive man. No matter how much she liked having him here to seduce and distract her.

"Ah." He came near enough that she could feel his body heat. His gaze roved her face. "Back to the solo feminine perfection you've become famous for."

Ignoring the melting sensation in her tummy, she acknowledged just as sassily, "Yes. Back to that."

Laugh lines appeared at the corners of his eyes. "Does your brand allow you to eat dinner?"

Generally? "If it's quick."

He handed over the bag of takeout, his fingers brushing hers. "Quick as your favorite southwestern chicken salad."

Her mouth watered.

The problem was, it had been such a long day and eating would make her sleepy. She couldn't afford to nod off. Not for another four or five hours yet, minimum. "Thank you," she said, putting it in the fridge. "I'll eat it later."

In the meantime, she appreciated his moral support. Not everyone would understand why she was running herself ragged to pursue a career in the big time. But Cade did.

He took in her tree, with its sparkling white lights, light blue glass ornaments, silver snowflakes and stars, and crystal medallions. "Wow. This is pretty."

Remembering all the times she had cheered him on in his career, happy he was now doing so for her, Allison returned to his side and surveyed the project with a professional eye. She yearned to take a time-out with him. A long, luxurious time-out. "It's not quite finished yet…"

He seemed stunned by her critique. "What's lacking?"

Her need to lean on him, just for a little while, increased by leaps and bounds. "A white chiffon tree skirt and a glass star tree topper." Both of which were nearby.

"I see."

She warmed at his lazy once-over.

His broad shoulders relaxed. "Well, I like it."

"Do you?" she bantered back. She would have assumed he would be more traditional.

"Mmm-hmm." He took her by the hand and drew her against his hard masculine length, so they were pressed up against each other in one long, tensile line. He gazed at her lips. "In fact, I like a lot of things…"

Sensation shimmered through her. His lower half tautened, too. Not sure she would be able to resist him much longer, she gave in to impulse and taunted softly, "Mighty confident, aren't you?"

He brushed the hair away from her face. The kind

of tenderness she'd always had trouble resisting radiating in his gaze, he nodded. "Oh, yeah."

Even professional athletes took breaks to recharge, midgame. Maybe this moment should be her seventh-inning stretch...

It could be part of her plan. A way to achieve her goal...

They were grown-ups, after all.

They could make love while still refuting the possibility of anything more.

In fact, Allison mused, maybe they'd even prefer it this way.

"The question is," she whispered, temptation running rampant inside her, "should you be that confident?"

Chapter Ten

Cade studied Allison's upturned face. Her lips were softly parted; her eyes were a glorious dark green. Her hair had been put into a messy knot on the back of her head, with strands escaping to curve against her pink sculpted cheeks. In that instant, she looked as if she wanted nothing more than to be kissed, and damn it all if he didn't want to kiss her, too.

His earlier decision to take everything nice and slow abandoned, he wrapped his arms around her waist and tugged her close. "Let's find out, shall we?" he growled, bending his head.

She rose up on tiptoe and pressed her breasts to

his chest. Her eyes dreamy, she lifted her lips to his. "Let's…"

The single softly spoken word was all the encouragement he needed. He lowered his mouth to hers. She smelled like an intoxicating blend of wintergreen, jasmine and woman. And she tasted just as sweet, her soft kiss as compelling as he remembered. Her body yielding. Not quite in surrender, but in *something…*

Wanting to make her his again, he slid a hand down her spine and back up again. He felt her melt against him a little more. Satisfaction roared through him, mingling with the excitement and the anticipation. Tunneling his hands through her hair, he worked to deepen the kiss. Again and again, until she leaned all the way in and ardently explored his lips in return.

Resolving to make her realize just how much they could have, if she gave him the opportunity, he slipped his hands beneath her shirt. Then, running his thumbs over the crests of her breasts, savoring the feel of her in his arms, he let her know with every kiss and caress how much he wanted to be there for her now. How much he *cared*.

Determined to give her all the pleasure she deserved, he backed her purposefully to the wall, unbuttoning and unzipping as they went. His palms and fingertips eased beneath the cloth and made a leisurely tour of her delectable body. "Damn, but I've missed you, Allison," he rasped.

"Right back at you, slugger," she moaned with a soft sigh of acquiescence, trembling when he found the sensitive place between her thighs. Desire shot through him, and he moved his mouth to her breasts, nibbling and sucking through the lace of her bra. Her skin grew hot, and her eyes darkened with lust, as lower still, the satin of her panties grew damp.

He loved her like this. All soft and womanly. Rocking against him. So restless and open to everything, so willing to let him take the lead.

Wedging his knee between her legs, he brought one leg up, so she could ride his thigh. She writhed against him, rubbing, seeking, her tongue tangling with his. Her breath caught even more as he found her center, remembering all too well exactly what she liked, stroking her and finding the wet, velvety heat. Quivering, her hands found the waistband of his jeans, his zipper, then slid inside to cup him. Another thing he loved about her. She wasn't shy about letting him know how much she wanted him, too. "Upstairs?" he murmured, wary that if they stayed where they were, doing what they were, it might all go by too fast.

Her eyes glimmered as she regarded him breathlessly. Seeming to remember that when he was with her, he liked to really take his time.

The flush of excitement in her cheeks deepened.

She smiled mischievously. "Bed sounds really good about now…"

He chuckled and let her take him by the hand and go up to the second floor. Half the size of the first, it was divided into three large rooms. A bedroom with a queen-sized bed and gorgeous silk chaise. An en suite bathroom with a luxurious shower, claw-foot soaking tub, mirrored sink and sit-down vanity. And, last but not least, a closet decked out to resemble a small high-end boutique.

"Wow," he said. She had done well for herself. Better than he could have imagined.

Allison had wanted to impress Cade. Wanted him to know just how well she had done on her own. That, unlike before, when she'd thought the only way they could ever be together was if they were madly in love and destined for a forever future with each other, she knew now she could live in the moment. At least with him.

Because the moment was safer.

It had no heavy implications.

And could carry them both through the otherwise incredibly lonesome holidays…

"Think of it as my lab," she quipped, determined to keep this light and easy, no matter what her still-humming body craved. Wanting to make it clear she knew exactly what she was doing here, she guided him back to her bedroom and over to her bed.

He regarded her like a man who always got what he wanted. And what he wanted right now was *her*.

"I could go for that."

Heart pounding and nipples tightening, she reached for the buttons on his shirt. The trouble was, she wanted him, too. Had from the first moment he had shown up and teased her into paying attention to him again. "I knew it wouldn't be long before you got into the game," she taunted him right back, resolved to stay in full control of the passion flowing unchecked between them.

"Ah. Baseball metaphors." He stripped down to just his boxer briefs. And there was no doubt how much he desired her. "Darlin', you do aim to please."

Allison kept her gaze high and ignored the racing of her heart. Wow, he sure looked good. All hard sinew and satiny skin.

"And be pleased in return." Remembering how much he liked her hair loose and sexy, she released it from the knot on the back of her head.

He grinned as she let it fall about her shoulders. Sauntered closer still. And then his lips were on hers, drawing her in, and she was as lost in him as she had ever been.

Allison knew passion alone couldn't hold a couple together. But tonight, the red-hot lust they felt was what was bringing her and Cade back to each other, at least as friends with occasional benefits, and right now, she needed that.

Needed *him*.

No one had ever made her feel the way he did. Or ever would. So why not give herself an early Christmas present and let down her guard? Forget all the reasons that had been keeping them apart. And still might. And just go for the real happiness that had been eluding her during the eight long years they'd been apart...

Together, they tumbled down onto her bed. She gasped as he tugged her to the edge of the mattress and dropped down between her spread knees. He eased off her jeans. Hooked his thumbs in her panties, drew them down, then off, burying his face in the most feminine part of her.

"Cade..." She caught his head, quivering now.

"Shh..." he whispered, running his thumb along the delicate seam. "I have a lot to finish here."

She laughed softly as he dropped gentle kisses, determined to help her find the release she sought. Unable to help herself, she gave him full rein, her body responding with a tidal wave of lust, all her inhibitions and worries floating away. And still he stroked the silky nub and eased inside her, letting the fluttering of his tongue entice her to open for him even more. Until there was no more pretending that she wasn't falling for him all over again, no more holding back, and she came apart in his hands.

He held her until the aftershocks passed. Pausing only long enough to grab the condom he carried in his wallet, he claimed her once again. Sliding between her thighs. Lifting her hips. Kissing her even as he eased inside her. Making her realize just how badly she had wanted to make love with him again.

Lost in the pleasure, she shut her eyes and let him kiss her senseless. Going deeper, slower still. His hips pressing down on hers, he took her masterfully and the climax she'd felt earlier came roaring back. She rose to meet him, savoring his heat and his hardness. Trembled and clenched around him. He dived deep. A cry of exultation rose in her throat. And then there was no more holding back. She surrendered to him the way she always had. With fierce abandon and incredible need, they catapulted into mind-bending pleasure.

Afterward, they lay wrapped in each other's arms. As much as Allison wanted to pretend they could stay locked in this erotic fantasy forever, she knew they couldn't. Aware she wasn't anywhere near as in control of this situation as she'd wanted to be, she forced herself to shake off the delicious sense of well-being that came from such an earth-shattering release. Looked at the clock beside her bed. Groaned. "Nine o'clock. I've got to get moving."

He rose, too. All confident male. "What can I do to help?"

Mischief glimmering in her eyes, she gestured at his abundant sex and shimmied into her red satin

panties and matching lace-trimmed bra. "Not distract me?"

"Seriously." He sighed, his body as ready for more
as hers was.

"I am serious." She reached for her corduroy shirt
and slid her arms through the sleeves. "If you stay
here, all half-naked, I'm not going to want to do anything but climb right back in bed with you." An act
that would tempt her to make this into more than the
strictly physical release it had been.

She had done that once with him.

Entered into a relationship that was ill-fated from
the beginning. She was not doing it again. No matter how sentimental she felt during the Christmas
holidays.

Cade had sensed Allison's emotional withdrawal
coming, long before she eased from the bed and
began to dress. Even when they'd been together,
she'd had a wall around her heart. Kept in place for
all sorts of reasons, the least of which was her refusal
to truly let herself depend on anyone.

"And I still have so much to do," she continued
with a brisk smile.

Wanting this to end well, he began to dress, too.
"I thought you just had two things to add to the tree
downstairs," he said companionably.

She surreptitiously watched him pull on his boxer
briefs. When he caught her admiring his physique,

a faint blush highlighted her cheeks. "But I haven't done the short explanatory video that goes with every post yet." She went into the bathroom and emerged, still blushing as she ran a brush through her hair.

Glad she wasn't as immune to what had just transpired between them as she pretended to be, he pulled on his jeans. "I thought those were only a couple of minutes."

She handed him his shirt. "Yes, but I have to look perfect."

He let his gaze rove her love-tousled state. "Trust me, there is nothing not to like about you right now." From her glowing skin, bright eyes and rosy lips... she was gorgeous.

She studied him incredulously. "You want me to do the video just like this?"

"I do." It would be one more way to remember this night.

Her eyes were dark and unwavering on his. "Okay. Sure." She put on the jeans and wool socks she'd been wearing when he arrived. "Let's go." She tugged on her boots and he followed her downstairs.

Abruptly all business, she added the tree topper and skirt, then switched on the video camera with a timer that had already been set up on a tripod. While he watched, she went through the basics of tree decorating for single women. Finishing with, "The most important thing to remember here is the only person you have to please is you. Until next time, merry holiday season!" She smiled into the camera a long moment, then made a slashing motion in front of her face. "Cut."

"That was great," he said admiringly. "Absolutely perfect in one take." She looked amazing, too. Not so much like the uptight perfectionist from *My Cottage Life*, but the Allison of old. The Allison he had fallen hard for. And kept right on wanting, for the last eight years...

Oblivious to his thoughts, she said, "I've been doing how-to videos a long time."

"How many have you made?" he asked curiously.

"Over a thousand."

She really was ambitious. "Are they all available on your website?"

"No. I edited out the ones that weren't perfect."

Of course she had.

She looked yearningly at the fridge, where she'd put the grilled chicken salad he'd picked up for her.

He crossed to her side. "Want to take a dinner break?"

She splayed her hands across his chest, holding him at bay. "Um. Not yet."

He wondered when she would allow herself to eat. "You want to head for Sarabeth and Shawn's to finish the other tree?"

Looking thoughtful, Allison nodded. "I need to pack up my video camera and stuff first, though. So why don't you go ahead and I'll meet you there?"

* * *

Although Allison had said she was good with their lovemaking, Cade could see the inner conflict reflected on her face. She might not want to say it, but she was probably already wondering if their return to physical intimacy had been a step in the wrong direction. He was wondering that, too. He had wanted her to be sure of his feelings for her before they made love again, so she would know deep in her heart and her soul that she could trust him not to hurt or neglect her this time around. But she'd wanted him and he'd wanted her, and it had felt right, so they'd gone with it. And now, predictably, she was having second thoughts about the wisdom of their actions.

Had she not been facing pressing work deadlines, he would have taken her back to bed and eased any of her worries about their pending reconciliation there.

But between her professional obligations and their babysitting duties, that wasn't going to be possible tonight, so he did as she asked, promised to meet her in a bit and headed out.

His three sisters were waiting for him. They surveyed him en masse. "You know, if you want to pretend nothing is simmering between you and Allison, you're going to have to work a lot harder to wipe that sparkle out of your eyes," Faith teased.

"Or at least pretend you're not having such a good time playing Mommy and Daddy with her," MacKenzie said.

He'd have to be an Oscar-worthy actor to pull that off. Cade sent his siblings a bemused smile. "You didn't see us together." So there was no way they could know the depth of his feelings for Allison.

Jillian mugged comically. "True. But we heard you telling stories about the two of you handling the quadruplets' antics out at the ranch today. And it was clear that you and Allison are working great as a team. Which, I have to say, was not a surprise to any of us."

"What do you mean by that?" Cade asked, noting that the only thing Allison had on the "family tree" she was supposed to be decorating thus far were the lights he'd helped her string the evening before.

Faith stood. "It means you've never loved anyone but Allison."

"And vice versa." MacKenzie joined Faith in the foyer.

"You know I don't need your matchmaking," Cade pointed out wryly, gathering up their coats.

Jillian wagged a finger his way. "Just don't wait too long to tell her how you really feel."

"Or you could lose this chance to reconcile," Faith agreed.

Cade realized that. He also knew Allison was a great deal more of a perfectionist than he was. She liked to analyze everything before proceeding and make a detailed plan for the future. Hence, she was going to need time to process the shift in their relationship. And understand that while her star might be rising, his was fading. He wasn't the hotshot ballplayer she had fallen in love with. A lot of changes lay ahead of them. Changes that they would have to be able to navigate well together, if they were to ever really make a go of it, long-term. He didn't want to ever disappoint her or let her down again, the way he had in the past.

Pressuring her into something she wasn't quite ready for would be doing just that.

Even more important, he did not want Allison having to deal with this familial interference, and since she might be arriving anytime, he thanked his sisters for all their help, cut the conversation short and showed them the door.

The only problem was, Allison didn't arrive shortly thereafter. It was another hour and a half before she showed up. And when she did, she wasn't in the casual clothing she'd been wearing when he left, but in one of those fancy outfits she liked to wear when taping segments for her blog. It looked like she had done her hair and makeup, too. She had the dinner he'd brought her and put it—so far untouched—into the fridge. He hoped for later.

"Hey. I was beginning to get worried about you," he said, lacing an easy arm about her waist.

Looking more stressed out than he could ever recall seeing her, she wedged an elbow between them, firmly keeping him at bay. "I had to redo the video for my 'single woman' tree. And I'm going to have to make one for the family tree while the kids are sleeping, too. So…" She gave him a pointed look, seeming anxious to get to it.

"You really redid that video?" he asked, aware that if that was going to be the case, they probably should have waited to make love. Rather than make her to-do list longer, her work life more cumbersome.

She shrugged, ruefully accepting the complications that had ensued. "I had no choice."

He quirked a brow.

"My hair wasn't exactly right and I didn't have makeup on."

Yet she had looked gorgeous.

"My blog devotees would have complained I wasn't living up to my…brand…" She said the last word reluctantly.

His gaze trailed over the hollow of her throat, past her lips to her pretty dark green eyes. "Which is perfection."

She inclined her head. Looked even more uncomfortable. "Listen, Cade, I enjoyed…earlier…but I don't really have time to talk."

She was as determined to keep him at arm's length as he was to get close to her again. Convincing her they hadn't rushed into anything was going to be tough. Especially since he had his own niggling doubts, given the way she was currently freezing him out. Fortunately, he knew, even if Allison didn't just yet, that he was more than up to the task. All he had to do was make sure, in the long run, that she gave them the second chance they deserved.

Resolved to be as patient as was required in this situation, he said, "And you really don't want or need my help right now." He guessed where this was going.

She sighed, every emotional barrier firmly back in place. "I really don't."

Cade tried not to take the rejection personally as he set off on one last late-night stroll with Zeus. He looked down at the dog at his side. "It's not as if I didn't do pretty much the same thing to her when we were a couple," he told his canine pal, feeling disappointed nevertheless. "I left her plenty of times, even right after making love, to get in one more batting practice or workout."

Zeus's ear pricked forward, giving Cade the equivalent of a canine scowl of reproof.

"And it got worse after that," Cade admitted reluctantly, figuring maybe he deserved this for all his past sins.

"As time went on, it wasn't just practice. I abandoned any plans we had made to spend time together, to go and give an interview with the campus newspaper or a local sports reporter."

Zeus huffed and went to the closest mailbox to lift his leg.

"Yeah." Cade accepted the commentary on his past behavior. "I was a selfish ego-driven jerk back in those days. To the point I can only imagine the things I would have left her to go and do had she and I still been together when I hit the big time."

Zeus ambled on down the sidewalk beside him.

Cade looked down at him and, enjoying the brisk cold of this December night, continued chatting. "So it was at that point in my career journey that Allison saw the writing on the wall and jumped ship, rather than endure any more solo misery."

Letting that happen had been the biggest mistake of his life. "I could take what might be a pretty big hint from her and do the same to her right now," Cade continued.

Zeus stopped at the end of the block, studied a sparkling display of Christmas lights. Then did an abrupt about-turn and headed back in the direction they had come. "Trying to tell me not to be impulsive?" he asked.

Because really, where would that get him and Allison? Alone again? When they had just begun to really find their way back to each other?

No, he decided, as Zeus headed even more briskly down the walk to the home they'd left. Where the woman of his dreams still was.

"I'm going to be smarter this time," Cade told Zeus, softly but firmly. "Not let my ego get in the way. Or make the same old mistakes. If she needs me to be understanding and accommodating, then I promise you this, buddy—I'm going to be more so than she ever dreamed," Cade vowed, as Zeus's tail began to wag. "And we'll see where things go from there."

Chapter Eleven

"You pulled an all-nighter, didn't you?" Cade said the following morning when Allison opened the front door, wearing the same outfit she'd had on when he left her shortly before midnight the evening before. Her hair, gloriously down before, was now pulled into a tight, messy knot at the nape of her neck. Her lips were bare and she looked tired around the eyes, yet her nonstop energy and ambition shone through anyway.

"Don't be silly. I got two hours of sleep."

"Two hours," he echoed her, walking inside, carrying a Sugar Buzz bakery bag of goodies.

"So, I'm fine." She shut the front door, flashed a

crisp professional smile that bore none of the intimate affection they had shown each other the evening before.

Cade knew it would take time—and privacy—to woo her. He echoed her cordial tone. "Mmm-hmm."

"However, I do think it might be wise if you were the one behind the wheel when we take the girls to preschool drop-off this morning."

"We?" He still liked the sound of that. The picture it brought of their potential future.

Her lips twisted. "Better to be cautious, don't you think?"

Where everyone was concerned. "I do." Perhaps it wouldn't be as hard as he thought to get close to her again. Especially now that she had finished her latest work task. Luxuriating in the subtle notes of her jasmine perfume, he let his glance drift over her. "Did you ever eat dinner?"

"I did." Together, they walked into the living room, being careful to avoid the hanging mistletoe. "Otherwise, I wouldn't have made it through the work I had to do. Thank you for that."

"You're welcome." He just wished she would let him do more, but one day at a time...

He stopped short of the "family tree" she had spent the wee hours of the morning decorating. Strands of white lights twinkled. Vintage wooden cranberry garlands were interspersed with red and green fabric bows and white, silver and gold ornaments. The tree skirt was a snowy white, and a beautiful angel sat atop the tree. It was very traditional and absolutely perfect in every respect. He imagined she'd done a lot of measuring to make certain. "Get your video completed for this one?"

Allison smiled proudly. "I posted them both simultaneously right before the girls woke up."

"I'm glad," he said softly.

She leveled an assessing gaze on him, kept it there, and he could have sworn, as the intimate moment drew out, she was thinking about kissing him again. Which was great, because that was what he was thinking about doing, too. Not as a preface to making love this time, but to show her what was in his heart.

He moved closer, just as footsteps sounded on the stairs. "Mr. Cade! Did you see what Miss Allison did?" Sienna declared accusingly. "She decorated our tree without us! While we were sleeping!"

"And she did it all wrong!" Jade agreed sulkily. "None of our special stuff is on there! Not even the ornaments we made at your mom and dad's ranch yesterday!"

Uh-oh, Cade thought.

No wonder she had looked so completely wrung out when he'd arrived.

What she had hoped would turn into a happy surprise had instead become a total disaster, at least as far as their four little matchmakers were concerned.

Allison held up both hands in surrender. She looked to him for support. "I told them I'd undo it, except for the lights, while they were at school, and we would start over when they got home this afternoon."

"That sounds like a plan to me," Cade said.

All four girls continued to pout.

"Now, how about you girls go upstairs and finish getting dressed, and then we can all make your school lunches together and maybe...just maybe—" he waved the Sugar Buzz bag in his hand "—give you a special treat to put in them."

Not surprisingly, the girls weren't that easily mollified. They glared at him and Allison. *"Fine!"* Amber said. Her sisters dramatically echoed the same and stomped back in the direction they'd come, pausing only to fling their hair and glare until they finally disappeared from view.

Zeus came over to stand beside Cade with a look that said he did not know how much more drama he could take. Had Cade not been so amused, he would have felt the same. He looked at Allison and murmured under his breath, "No fury like four women scorned?"

He felt her stiffen almost imperceptibly beside him. She punched him in the arm, looking harried and upset. "Fun-ny." Her pine-green eyes narrowed in consternation.

He set the bag on the kitchen island, then turned

to face her. "Seriously, I'll be around to help. Just don't forget that the carpet guys are supposed to be here around noon to put the carpet and padding back and collect the dehumidifier fan."

Looking abruptly as if her knees were about to buckle, she slid onto a stool. Gulping anxiously, she recalled, "We never did tell Sarabeth and Shawn what happened there."

With good reason, given their marital troubles and Shawn's accident. He waved off her concern and took the stool next to her. Enjoying the intimacy of them sitting knee to knee. "They'll be fine with it, since no harm no foul."

Clearly unconvinced, Allison bit her lip and looked up at him.

Ignoring the way the skirt of her dress had hiked up on her thighs, he kept his gaze on her face. "We'll just tell them when they get back so they can see for themselves it's all *fine*." He comically emphasized the last word.

She started giggling. Tears of levity blurred her eyes. "I'm about to get punchy," she warned.

Loving the sound of her laughter, he teased, "I thought you already did that." He rubbed his left arm as if it still smarted.

"Ha ha."

Allison slid off the stool, bumping knees with him in the process, then looked around as if wondering what she should do next. Another sign of how tired she was. This woman always knew exactly what to do next.

"Let me feed Zeus his breakfast—" Cade rose, towering over her "—and then I'll help you with the lunches."

She curled her toes beneath her tights, having lost her shoes somewhere along the way. "I already fed him."

Zeus wagged his tail, knowing he was being talked about and not averse to a second meal by mistake, either.

Cade bent down to pet the dog. Then, seeing he could probably use a little more water, he took the bowl over to the sink for a refresh. "You?" He tossed a look at her over his shoulder. "Miss I-don't-think-I-like-dogs?"

Cheeks pinkening, Allison made a seesawing motion with her hand. "He's growing on me." She bent down to pet him, her dress riding up well past her knees again.

Feeling the telltale stirring of his body, Cade shifted his gaze away. "Zeus is a very loyal fella." He carried the filled water bowl back.

"And patient and loving." Allison gave the Lab's silky black-and-white face another stroke, then rose a little more awkwardly than usual.

Another sign of her bone-deep fatigue.

Cade put out a hand to steady her, cupping her elbow as she straightened.

"Which is exactly what you need?" he guessed. Especially around the holidays. Love. Patience. And loyalty. Lots of it.

Her eyes turned misty. "Sometimes lately, yes, I do think I might need to get a dog of my own to keep me company."

She needed a lot more than that, he thought.

"Although I'm not sure how that would work with my brand. Since a lot of single women prefer cats."

"Do you?" he challenged.

The color in her cheeks deepened. "No, but that's not exactly the point."

He frowned back at her. "It's exactly the point."

She clearly didn't agree.

"You have to make yourself happy, Allison."

Temper flared in her green eyes. "Is that so?"

He grinned, loving it when he got under her skin. "It's absolutely so." He leaned in, thinking now was the perfect time to steal a kiss...

"Mr. Cade!" A shrill four-year-old voice sounded behind him. He turned to see Amber standing there, her hands on her hips, her three sisters right behind her. "That is not where the mistletoe is!" she scolded. "You cannot kiss unless you are under the mistletoe."

Wow. What a moody crew they had.

"Is this what they mean when they say estrogen positive?" he asked Allison solemnly.

She burst into laughter. And this time could not stop, even when the girls asked her why.

Hazel stared. "*What* is wrong with Miss Allison?"

Cade got the lunch bags out of the fridge and began doling out the individually wrapped Christmas sugar cookies for the girls to add to their lunches as a special treat. "She's punchy."

Sienna nodded. "Very punchy."

"What's punchy?" Jade asked.

"It's what happens when you don't get enough sleep," Cade explained, as Allison wiped the tears of laughter from her eyes. "So remember that, girls. Always go to bed on time!"

Allison rolled her eyes, looking both impressed and amused. "Nice way to slide in a life lesson."

Cade thought so, too. Maybe he was more suited to being a parent than he had imagined. Allison, too...

She smiled at him over the kids' heads. Aware he hadn't felt this happy or content in a long time, even when he'd been playing ball, he smiled back. "Let's get this show on the road, ladies!" He found their coats and backpacks, and together, he and Allison herded them all out to the SUV.

The drive to school was as lively as ever, with the girls alternately arguing with each other, singing songs from their upcoming Christmas performance and asking a barrage of questions.

"Miss Allison, did you call our mommy so you can find out where our *real* Christmas decorations are?" Sienna asked, as Cade turned into the long curving drive in front of the preschool to wait their turn in line.

Regretting having tried to combine an HITN assignment with her babysitting duties, Allison promised, "I'm going to talk with your mommy before you get home from school." Or at least she would try. Between the time difference, the girls' school and her work schedule, it would not be easy.

"Okay, but we have got to have them, or our tree will *still* not look right," Jade said, unclasping her seat belt prematurely.

"Girls," Cade warned in the rearview mirror, as another latch audibly unsnapped. "We're still driving."

"Mommy's Suburban isn't moving," Hazel pointed out, unfastening hers, too. Albeit a little more discreetly.

"It's temporarily stopped," Cade said. "For traffic. We'll move again in a second…"

"Re-latch your seat belts," Allison directed, beginning to feel like the *Mom* to Cade's *Dad*…

To Allison's frustration, no one complied with her directive. Meanwhile, Amber eased hers off. Testing them, too.

Cade's brows lowered. "I mean it or I'm not moving forward," he said sternly. "And you know what that means. The Traffic Mommy is going to come back and scold us for not following the safety rules."

Experience had taught them the girls found it too embarrassing to be singled out in front of their peers. Four latches sounded. Followed by four loud sighs.

"Thank you," Cade said, sounding more like a veteran daddy than ever.

Suppressing a smile, Allison turned to look out her window, past the school, toward the street ahead. To her amazement, she could have sworn she saw the Angry Fan who had confronted Cade in the San Angelo mall. Except this time, he wasn't with that woman or sporting a goatee or wearing a Wranglers baseball cap. Instead, he was wearing sunglasses, a Stetson and a shearling coat. Phone pressed to his ear, he was climbing into a nondescript gray sedan and fumbling with the phone, which was resting against the top of the steering wheel.

Cade eased forward in the traffic line.

"Everything okay?" he asked her.

Allison nodded slowly, still trying to surreptitiously make sense of what she was seeing, without doing or saying anything that would alarm the girls.

Cade braked in front of the school.

"Oh, no, my shoe came off!" Sienna said in alarm.

The Traffic Mom opened the rear passenger door. Sienna started to cry in distress.

"Hang on. I'm coming to help!" Allison said, jumping out.

While the other girls climbed out of the Suburban with the help of the Traffic Mom, then were escorted to the school by another, Allison quickly got Sienna's sneaker on and the Velcro tabs fastened. "There you go," she said.

Still tearful, Sienna emerged from her car booster seat. Seeing she needed comfort, Allison opened her arms and gave the four-year-old a big hug. She bent her head and pressed a kiss onto the top of her head. "You're okay now, right?"

Sienna nodded and clung to her. "Thank you, Miss Allison," she whispered.

"Anytime." Allison hugged her back and unexpectedly felt herself tearing up, too. Was this what life with a big family was like? Had she been missing out by declaring she wasn't interested in having a husband and children? And most important, was it possible it wasn't too late after all for her to have everything she had once wanted? With Cade?

"You are really tired, aren't you?" Cade remarked as he drove away from the school.

"Why do you say that?" Allison asked, looking at the place where the Angry Fan had been. Except there was no vehicle there now.

Was she seeing things?

She shook her head. The reality was, if there had been a stalker anywhere near the school, one of the other parents certainly would have picked up on it, gotten a license plate number and reported it.

Cade probably would have noticed, too.

Had he not been busy watching traffic and the unfolding drama of the unlatched seat belts and falling-off sneaker.

Briefly, she told him what she thought she had seen. "But there is nothing there now, so I don't know." Frowning, he looked over at her. "I think I am just overtired," she admitted with a telltale quaver. First, she had seen trouble where there might have been none and then been moved to tears by a little girl's hug.

He reached over and touched a tear still trembling on her lower lash. "Is that all that's going on with you this morning?"

Not about to tell him how much she was beginning to realize she wanted a family of her own, she lifted a dismissive hand. "Nothing a bowl of cereal and a nap won't cure." It was certainly possible this was all due to too much job pressure, low blood sugar and lack of sleep!

He looked over at her, as protective as ever. "Want to go back to your place?"

Allison smiled. Sometimes it was good to be taken care of. Especially by an incredibly kind and sexy man. And it was Christmas, after all. The season of giving… "If you don't mind driving me. Yes, I would."

He reached across the console to companionably squeeze her knee. "My lady's wish is my command."

Another wave of heat swept through her. The kind

she would have felt if they'd had the time to make love again the evening before. Attempting to keep her mind on their repartee, instead of the sizzling chemistry between them, she murmured, "Feeling chivalrous this morning?"

He flashed a mysterious smile. "I'm always chivalrous when I'm around you. Haven't you noticed?"

She had. It was what had made breaking up with him so hard years ago. "What are your plans for the day?"

He sobered. "I need to do some prepping for an interview with the school board and superintendent tomorrow morning."

Brought back to reality, Allison asked, as they arrived at her house and went in together, "How do you prepare for something like that?"

Cade fell into step beside her as they traversed the walk to her front porch. "The Q and A part you really don't because that should come straight from your heart. But the written lesson plan they're going to want to see for the way I intend to coach." He released his light grip beneath her elbow. "That, I'm going to have to pull from my college sports education days."

She shot him a look over her shoulder, feeling a little bereft now that he had stopped touching her. "You still have all that stuff?"

He shoved his hands in his pockets and watched

her turn the key. "Oh, yeah. I knew this day would come."

He'd never said as much to her. But then, years before, they hadn't really talked about the future when it came to what they wanted. Only the present. The possibility of high salaries. And fame. Which he'd had. And she was well on her way to getting. Although perhaps not major-league-baseball-level money or fame...

Cade took off his jacket and made himself right at home. More damning still, she couldn't say she minded. It felt right, somehow, having him around like this again. And even better to have someone take care of her for a change.

"So. What do you want for breakfast?" He held up a staying hand. "And don't say cereal. You need something more substantial after being up all night, something with plenty of protein." Their hips and shoulders bumped as they met up near the stove.

She remembered the few dishes he could manage not to burn. "Like scrambled eggs with cheese?"

He folded his arms across his chest, the hunger in his eyes matching hers. "Sounds good to me," he admitted in that rough-tender voice she loved.

He looked good to her. All freshly shaven and showered. In a knit shirt that clung to his broad shoulders and molded to his hard pecs and flat abs. Jeans that did the same thing for his hips and legs. He'd always been an athlete. Now he was starting to show signs of being a great dad, as well as good husband material.

And that, she was surprised to find out, was incredibly sexy.

"Um…" Pushing aside her unexpectedly romantic thoughts, she inhaled. And tried not to think about how much she needed to touch him. "To me, too." Averting her glance, lest he see too much of what she was thinking and feeling, she brought out the carton of eggs, butter and a block of cheddar from the fridge.

"I'll take it from here," he said.

"Ah. The perks of dating an athlete." She slid her weary body onto a stool and rested her chin on her upturned palm. "They're always hungry. Most of them know how to cook at least a few things reasonably well." At least she hoped that was still the case. "And they always know what you should eat."

He set the skillet on the stove, then came around the island. He swiveled her stool, so her back was to the counter. And planted a hand on either side of her, trapping her in place. He grinned, slow and sexy, and kept his eyes on her face. Waggling his brows, he asked, "Are we dating?"

A tremor of desire slid through her. All she could think—or want—was to make love with him again. Telling herself to slow down, lest he shatter her heart all over again, she leaned back slightly. "Cade…"

He leaned in closer. His gaze drifted over her hair,

cheeks, mouth and throat before returning with slow deliberation to her eyes. "Is it possible we could?"

The romantic side of her wanted to say yes. *Heck, yes!* But the way they had crashed and burned before made her hesitate. She didn't want to exert any expectations on them. Or take them out of the moment… which was turning out to be pretty darned good…

Deciding it would be best to avoid going down a road that might lead to conflict, she merely tilted her head, splayed her hands across his shirtfront and admitted, "Right now we just have to get through the week. Make it until Sarabeth and Shawn get home from Switzerland…"

He straightened and gave her a long, steady look before he moved away. "Then we will talk about this," Cade promised firmly.

They would have to. She knew that. She just didn't know what she would say.

"Mmm, that was scrumptious," Allison said half an hour later, as they finished up their cheesy scrambled eggs, toast and fresh fruit.

It was ironic. In their college days, he had always been extremely good to her when he was there. The problem had been that he hadn't been around enough. And they had both known that complication was only going to exacerbate when he turned pro.

Now he was suddenly with her constantly. In a way he never really had been before. But she didn't trust it to last. Not if her career took off. Or his did again, too. And that could happen.

"Another cup of decaf for your thoughts," he teased.

She rose, her knees still feeling slightly unsteady with bone-deep fatigue, and said the first thing that came to mind. "Your cooking has come a long way from your college days."

He preened comically. "Hasn't it?"

"And modest, too!"

"Hey." He hooked his arm about her shoulders and brought her close to his side. "If the compliment fits..."

She laughed softly. Now that she had eaten, she wanted nothing more than to sleep. But there were still chores to be done.

He caught the direction of her glance. His gaze turned warm, possessive. "I'll do the dishes. Let's get you to bed."

Allison drew a bolstering breath as her heart hammered in her chest. "You don't have to do that."

"Lead you to bed? Yeah, I'm afraid I do. You're a temporary mom now." He stepped behind her to knead the tense muscles of her neck and shoulders. "You have to rest when the opportunity presents itself. Otherwise, you won't have the energy to help with the girls later."

She leaned into his luxuriant touch. "True." She pivoted to face him and slayed him with her best I-can-handle-damn-near-anything look. "But I think I know where my bedroom is."

"Good." Ignoring her declaration of independence, he flashed the seductive grin that always melted her from the inside out. "That makes two of us."

Giving her no further chance to protest, he wrapped his arm about her waist and cuddled her close as they moved up the stairs and into the master suite that took up the entire second floor of the cottage. He stopped next to the bed. "Need pajamas?"

Did she?

Suddenly, all the reasons she'd had for slowing down seemed completely irrelevant. It was Christmastime, after all. They were both single and unattached. Both feeling immensely attracted to, and in need of comfort from, the other person.

Not sure she wanted to continue to fight the desire that had been plaguing her since they had started spending time together again, she took the cell phone out of her pocket, shut off the sound and set it on the bedside table.

"You're taking your role as protector very seriously." And she had to admit, she always had loved his innate gallantry. Never more so than right now.

The twinkle in his eyes intensified. "Is that a yes or a no?"

Decision made…she was giving this gift of time and togetherness to the both of them…she tugged the hem of his shirt from the waistband of his jeans. "It's a not right now…"

Catching her hand, he kissed the back of it. Their eyes locked. The mixture of desire and need told her all she wanted to know.

"Careful what you wish for, darlin'," he whispered, kissing her cheek, her temple, the sensitive spot just beneath her ear.

Aware she had never felt so cherished and adored as she did when she was with him, Allison brushed her lips across his and felt his body harden all the more. He tasted so good. So deliciously male. "Mmm. Speaking of wishes…" Hand hooked playfully in the waist of his jeans, she tugged him into the adjacent bathroom. A place that had never been properly christened until now. "What I wish for now is a nice hot shower. And although you appear to already have had one this morning, you are more than welcome to join me."

His laugh was low and husky. He eased the zipper of her dress down. She shimmied out of it, then her tights. Clad in bra and panties, she turned to start the water. By the time she'd adjusted the temperature, he was stripped down to the buff. He reached behind her to unclasp her bra. Drew it off. Helped her dispense with her panties. She stepped into the shower. With a very slow and sexy smile, he joined her under the spray.

His skin was hot. The water was warm. Her body was on fire.

He touched her erect nipples, bent his head and kissed her, wet and deep. Then slowly and tenderly until she wrapped her arms about him and moved impatiently against him.

She quivered as he drew her against his male perfection. She felt the length of him, so hot and hard. Then he was reaching for the body wash. Pumping it into his palms, he spread the silky liquid over her shoulders, across her breasts, down her tummy and between her thighs. She arched at the stroke of his fingers, the rubbing ministrations of his palms. And then he was turning her, attending to the expanse of back between her shoulder blades, down her spine, over the curve of her buttocks.

Sensation shimmered through her as he continued down to her thighs. Past her knees. And still water sluiced over her, over him. Suds sliding onto their feet. Finished, he brought her against him. "Feeling better?"

A shaky breath escaped her. "Much."

"Good."

And still he took his time, holding her close under the spray. Kissing and touching while she trembled in response, her flesh swelling to fill his palms. Bending her backward over one arm, he kissed and caressed her breasts, his fingers grazing from base to tip, his tongue laving the tight buds.

When she could take it no more, he parted her legs, then rubbed and stroked. She caressed him in turn, moving her fingers lightly over the length of him, then back again until he, too, was on the verge.

"I don't want to come without you, not this time," she whispered shakily.

He exited the shower long enough to retrieve a condom. She helped him roll it on, and then he settled her against the wall. She held on to his shoulders and wrapped her legs around his hips. And then they were kissing again. Ravenously. Until he was throbbing and she was wet and open. She moaned as he slid home. Intent on giving them what they both needed. Thrusting. Taking. Sending her over the edge and going right with her in a way that was so wild and perfect it stole her heart.

As the aftershocks faded, and Allison drifted to sleep, Cade held her close, aware he hadn't felt this content or at peace in years.

That wasn't surprising, of course.

The two of them had started dating in high school. Continued through four years of college. Moving in together and sharing an apartment for the last two.

He had taken her for granted then. Thinking she would always be there for him. And even though he had sensed she was increasingly unhappy, toward the end, he had still been surprised when she'd broken up with him and moved out.

He had expected her to forgive him and come back. It was why he had hired her to decorate his first home.

When she hadn't, he had discovered what it was like to have half your soul torn away.

The rigors of playing professional baseball had filled up his hours. And he had invested everything in the highs and lows of victory and defeat.

But he had always missed her.

Always dreamed about her.

Always thought…someday…they'd find their way back together.

Now they had.

At least for another four or five days.

Was that going to be enough to fully pique her interest and regain her trust? Show her what they could enjoy if they only gave each other a no-holds-barred second chance?

He didn't know.

He could only hope…

And though he wanted nothing more than to stay with her for the rest of the morning, and sleep with her wrapped in his arms, that wasn't going to be possible, either. He had dishes to finish up, an interview to prep for and carpet restoration workers to meet up with. All before the quadruplets were ready to be picked up from pre-K at three that afternoon.

So he eased from the bed, dressed quietly and left her a note, asking her to call him when she woke.

Remembering she had turned the ringer off before they made love, he looked down at her phone. Normally, he would have just left it off. Let her sleep uninterrupted. But they had kids they were caring for. Shawn and Sarabeth overseas. And the job of her dreams in the offing. So he did what she would have done had she had the opportunity before she drifted off. He turned the sound back on. And hoped that whatever came next would only bring them closer.

Chapter Twelve

Allison's cell phone chimed. Over and over again. Pushing out of the fog of sleeping at an unfamiliar time of day, she struggled to get up. Saw Laurel Grimes's caller ID on-screen. She grabbed the phone and answered the call from the HITN producer. "Hey, Laurel." She attempted to sound cheerful and awake.

"Glad I caught you," Laurel said. "Both trees were spectacular. And a lot easier for our viewers to emulate than the ones Jennifer Moore posted on *City Lights.*"

Allison appreciated the compliment, but she had been trying not to think about what her competitor might or might not be doing. It was enough to simply concentrate on her own tasks. "I'm glad you liked them," Allison said, stifling a yawn. Wondering where Cade had gone, and if he still felt as relaxed with the aftereffect of making love as she did. "So what is next?"

"Your take on a yuletide tradition. It can be anything as long as it's related to house decor."

Brought back to reality, Allison was all business once again. "No problem. When do you want it?"

"We'd like to see it posted on your blog by nine o'clock tomorrow morning," Laurel said.

"Will do." They said goodbye. Her mind already on the task ahead, Allison headed for the shower. An hour later, she was over at Shawn and Sarabeth's home with Cade and three workers from the restoration company, who were busy reinstalling the carpet in the upstairs hallway where it had previously flooded.

Cade rose from the dining room, where it seemed he had been busy putting together his coaching plan. "Hey," he said, coming near enough to give her a quick hug. "I was hoping you'd get a little more rest than that."

She leaned into his warmth, realizing all over again how tall he was, how smokin' hot. It didn't seem to matter how temporary this situation they were in was or how ill-suited they had been for each other in the past. Whenever she looked into his eyes, she felt the fierce magnetic pull. She wanted him. *Desperately.* Even though they had just made love a few hours before…

She pushed aside the sensual memories of their time together and, for both their sakes, moved back slightly. "I need to get out the traditional decorations for the tree here, so they'll be all ready when the girls come home from school this afternoon. But I'm still waiting to hear from Sarabeth about where they are stored." She grinned as she saw an incoming FaceTime request from Sarabeth. "And speaking of perfect timing…"

She moved a slight distance away from Cade, as the work continued on the second floor, and accepted the request. Almost immediately, Sarabeth's face came onto the screen. She was still in the hospital, Shawn beside her. But she looked good, Allison noted in relief. Happy, even. "Hi, Sarabeth."

"Aren't you cheerful!" Sarabeth grinned.

"Did you get my message?" Allison asked.

"Yes. The decorations are in red and green storage boxes in the attic on the third floor."

"I'll go see if I can find them," Cade volunteered.

Allison touched his arm. "Thanks." He briefly covered her palm with his own, then moved off.

Sarabeth registered surprise. "The two of you are getting along."

Very well, as it happened. *Too well?* Allison wondered. Knowing it was unlike her to be so impulsive.

Usually, she weighed every pro and con and planned her life down to the very last detail. Aware her friend was waiting for an explanation, she said, "We decided to bury the hatchet and be friends again."

Shawn chuckled. "Just friends?"

Cade came back into the room, his arms full of storage boxes. "Found 'em, and yeah—" he turned to wink at Allison as he set them down "—just friends. So how are things going in Switzerland?"

Briefly, the couple gave them an update on Shawn's progress. Which was slow, but steady. Then turned to the latest on the school Christmas performance. "The girls are all supposed to wear red dresses on Thursday evening," Sarabeth said. "The ones from last year didn't fit, so I ordered identical new ones online before we left. They were supposed to arrive today, but I just got an email notice that they won't be delivered until tomorrow."

"That's Tuesday. Plenty of time."

"Here's where it starts to get tricky," Sarabeth cautioned. "They also need new white tights and black shoes. You can get those at the children's boutique in town. The problem is, the girls are going to have to go in and have their feet measured. And they really *hate* trying on new shoes."

Allison and Cade traded glances. He shrugged his broad shoulders affably. "I'm sure we will be able to handle it," Allison said.

Sarabeth looked less than convinced but nodded

in any case. "There's one more thing. We confirmed with Shawn's doctors this morning that there is no way we can make it home in time for the performance, so…we're going to miss it."

Uh-oh, Allison thought.

"The girls will likely be upset," Shawn said.

No kidding.

"They're used to me missing things," Shawn said. "Not Sarabeth. I told her she should think about getting an earlier flight, for their sake."

"No," Sarabeth interjected firmly. "I'm needed here. I'm not leaving you." She looked back at the phone. "I'm going to ask you not to tell them we won't be there until Thursday before the performance. The less time they have to stew about it, or feel disappointed about it, the less temper tantrums there will be."

Allison figured they were probably right. "We can do that," she said, while Cade slid a reassuring arm about her waist.

"But don't worry. You won't have to break the bad news to them. Shawn and I will do that on Thursday before the show. And we'll also ask you two to videotape it for us, so we can all watch it together when we get back, and I know they will like that."

"Sounds good," Allison said, breathing in Cade's cedarwood-and-soap fragrance.

"We'll call again when the girls are home from school," Sarabeth promised.

"Talk to you then." They hung up. Afraid if she stayed that close to him they would end up kissing again, Allison eased away from Cade. She recalled that shopping never had been his favorite thing. But these weren't normal circumstances. "Want to go shoe shopping after school?" she asked lightly.

His brow furrowed. "The girls are expecting to redecorate the tree."

"We could still do that or at least start it after dinner. I'm just afraid if we wait on the clothes and there's a glitch…"

The corners of his sensual lips quirked. "Like there might be when we're trying to buy four identical pairs of black shoes in a certain kid size?"

Glad she suddenly had his full attention, she admitted, "We'd have to go to San Angelo, and that'll be half an hour there, half an hour back."

He clamped his hands on her shoulders. The move forced her to look him straight in the eye. "You're right." He smiled, ready to get this errand done. "We'll just pick them up from school and go straight there, then."

Naturally, it wasn't as easy as that. "I don't want to go shoe shopping without my mommy." Jade pouted, refusing to get out of her car booster seat.

Sienna folded her arms across her chest. She also refused Allison's assistance. "Mommy always takes us."

"We will just wait," Hazel said, without a trace of her usual good humor.

"I want to go home and be with Zeus," Amber agreed.

"It won't take long," Allison promised, continuing to hold out her hand while the girls remained truculently in place.

"And you know why?" Cade flashed his most charming grin. He angled his thumb at the center of his chest and declared dramatically, "Because I bet I hate shopping almost more than your daddy does."

Jade grinned, and just like that, the spell was broken. She accepted Cade's hand out of the SUV. "No, you don't," she argued back merrily.

"'Cause nobody hates shopping more than our daddy!" Sienna added.

Not about to be left out, the other two quadruplets scrambled to get out of the SUV. Cade took the hands of Jade and Sienna while Allison captured Hazel's and Amber's. Together, they walked the sidewalk in downtown Laramie until they got to the children's boutique located next to Monroe's Western Wear.

"You'll have to tell me all about shopping with your daddy while we try on shoes," he soothed.

So they did. While they got measured. And tried on soft black ballet-style shoes, as well as black patent-leather Mary Janes, and glittery black slip-on shoes that, while uncomfortably stiff, also had the unfortunate habit of sliding off the heels of the girls' slender feet.

"What do you think?" the clerk asked.

Cade looked to Allison for a decision. "I think it's between the black ballet shoes—" which had an elastic inside edge for a better fit "—or the patent-leather Mary Janes," which had a buckle strap across the middle.

"I want the sparkly ones!" Jade said heatedly. Her three sisters quickly agreed.

Allison looked at Cade. The shoes were definitely the prettiest, but they would be hell to break in. And worse, wouldn't stay on for even two steps. Hence, they were an accidental trip or slip-and-fall waiting to happen. Not good, when all four girls were going to be on stage in front of all the parents, their own nowhere to be found. Not that they knew that yet...

Cade's dark brown eyes met hers, understanding that persuasion was needed. He pointed to the most comfortable. "I like these because they're the kind ballet dancers and princesses wear."

"Princesses wear sparkles!" Sienna declared.

And to Allison and Cade's dismay, they could not convince the girls otherwise.

Cade steered Allison to the side. "What do you think?"

Allison's emotions warred. Empathy won out. "That maybe, given everything else ahead of them—" like their parents not being there to see the performance "—that this is one battle we should let them win?"

Cade nodded and squeezed her hand in agreement.

Fortunately, the white tights were an easy purchase. Finished, they headed home.

Unfortunately, by then it was nearly dinnertime for the girls, which on school nights was around five or five thirty. Baths and pj's followed, and though they still had time to decorate the family tree, the girls were not the least bit interested in cooperating about that or anything else, it seemed. "I don't want to do it without Mommy." Hazel's lower lip trembled.

Sienna was near tears, too. "We need Daddy to put the ornaments on the tippy-top."

Allison wished they would let her comfort them. "Cade and I can help you."

Jade's lower lip shot out. "You already ruined it by putting the other stuff, instead of *our* stuff, on it."

Amber cuddled Zeus as if her life depended on it. Sorrowfully, she advised, "We don't want it to be ugly again, Miss Allison!"

Ugly? They thought what she had done was ugly? Now Allison was near tears.

Cade laced a hand about her waist. "Nothing like being overtired," he quipped. Unlike her, he was not the least bit surprised or upset. "Listen, girls, it's pretty late. Why don't we read some Christmas storybooks, and then see if we can FaceTime with your mommy and daddy?"

Finally, something Allison could do to help. "I'll see if I can get them," she said. She texted, asking if it was a good time for a chat. A minute later, Sarabeth and Shawn called. What followed was a horrendously long list of complaints. Mostly about Allison. Cade miraculously escaped unscathed.

Cade eased her away from the table where the girls were gathered around Sarabeth's laptop computer, emoting nonstop. "Let them get it all out," he said.

They were. Boy, were they ever. Still, things were a lot calmer when the conversation wrapped up. "Be good listeners for Allison and Cade," Sarabeth concluded.

The girls blew kisses and the call ended. "Time for teeth brushing and bedtime," Cade said.

The girls went upstairs obediently. Ten minutes later, all were beneath their covers. A short time after that, all were asleep, and Cade and Allison were on their way back downstairs.

"Sorry they gave you such a hard time tonight," he said.

She smiled her admiration. "You're so good with them."

He kissed the top of her head. "So are you."

It was hard to believe him about that. With a sigh, she went back into the kitchen, unsure whether to go after the half-folded load of laundry or the half-finished dishes. It was unlike her to leave so much undone. To be so…unsuccessful. Usually, everything she did now was perfect. To the point she'd been teased her blog should be called *My Perfect Life* instead of *My Cottage Life*. Every anxiety she'd ever had about one day having a family of her own came to the fore. "Maybe I'm not cut out for motherhood." She went into the laundry room and began putting the damp clothes from the washer into the dryer.

Cade stepped back to give her room to work. "I didn't know you were interested in motherhood."

It wasn't something they had ever talked about when they were dating. But then, they hadn't talked marriage, either. They'd been focused on college. Their careers.

She hadn't let herself think about it after they'd broken up, either.

He crossed his arms, waited, daring her to go on. So, of course, she did. She angled her chin at him. "I wasn't. But this week has me thinking."

"It has me thinking, too…"

The next thing she knew, she was backed up against the clothes dryer. He pulled her in close so she was nestled against him. It was the first time he'd held her since they'd made love. She luxuriated in the heat of his body and the desire in his eyes.

Tempted to kiss him again—for all the wrong reasons this time—she wiggled out of his hold and eased away, her spine stiff. She hated it when she felt like a failure. And there was no doubt she had let the girls down today. Despite all her best efforts. "You don't have to soothe my feelings." She picked up the clothes basket of clean laundry and carried it into the breakfast room. Where the supper dishes also waited.

Leaving the basket on the floor, she went to clear the table. He followed suit, too. "Isn't that what friends are for?"

Friends. She wanted so much more than that. Tears trembled once again.

He stepped in to load the dishwasher. "They were just giving you the business because they're mad at their mom for leaving them, and you're the closest thing to a mother figure that they have right now."

The coziness factor in the room increased ten-fold. "How do you know that?" She stepped in to help him.

His gaze roved over her, as if he were mentally calculating where and when they could next make love. "Because when I was a kid, I was an expert at the same thing."

"You? Mr. Charm." She tried to imagine him being that temperamental and cantankerous, but couldn't.

Briefly, he covered her hand with his own. "Hey. I wasn't all sunshine and roses."

Ignoring the sparks the contact generated, Allison tried not to drown in the molten depths of his espresso-brown eyes. "I don't think you're all sunshine and roses now."

Chuckling, he shot her a wry look. They finished wiping down the counters and stepped to the sink simultaneously to rinse their hands. As their shoulders touched, Allison gave in to curiosity and asked, "Who did you give a hard time?"

He handed her a towel. "Every foster parent I had, including Carol and Robert."

Figuring it wouldn't hurt to take a break, Allison took him by the hand and led him into the living room to sit on the sofa. "How many homes were you in?"

His gaze turned brooding. "Six, that first year."

Hard to imagine. "Why so many?" She searched his face.

He leaned forward, scrubbing his hands over his face. Then stood and began to pace. "I was angry that my parents went back in the house, after it was struck by lightning and caught on fire—when my brother Travis and I begged them not to go. And even more furious when the gas water heater ignited and blew up shortly thereafter, taking them and everything we owned with it."

Allison listened, aware he never talked about the tragic chain of events that had altered his world.

Sorrow tightened the planes of his face. "Then social services came in and split all eight of us kids up that very night. Moved us all to different homes."

"Oh, Cade…" Her heart went out to him.

"It was miserable and scary. And I lashed out, against every person who made me feel even a tiny bit safe. The same way the girls are lashing out at you right now."

"Because I make them feel safe?"

He returned to sit beside her. "In the way that their mom does, yes."

She turned to face him, her bent knee pressing against his rock-hard thigh. "Why not you, then? You're certainly acting like a dad." And a very good one at that.

He ran his finger over her jean-clad knee with the same reverence he used when they made love. "They're used to Shawn traveling a lot, so they don't depend on him for every little thing. Just like they don't depend on me for every little thing, either, because I'm not here 24/7, the way their mom usually is…and you have been."

Suddenly, it all began to make sense. "Except for yesterday, when I had to work," Allison said slowly.

He inclined his head. "Maybe that's what their pent-up anger today is all about."

"Maybe."

She shifted all the way onto his lap and he wound his arms around her. His gaze drifted over her fondly. "Feel better now?"

There was no disputing it. "You always make me

feel better." It was why she had missed him so much these last eight years.

He scored his thumb across her lower lip. "You mean that?"

Aware the fragility she had been feeling had faded, she gave him a look that spoke volumes. "Kiss me," she invited softly, "and see…"

With a grin, he lowered his head. Her breath caught and she closed her eyes. And then all was lost in the first thrilling touch of their lips. Yearning swept through her, and their tongues met in an explosion of heat and need, passion and tenderness. His masculinity was the perfect counterpoint to her femininity. His kindness a balm to her soul. A contented sigh rippled through her, followed swiftly by a lightning bolt of desire that started in her breasts and exploded like holiday fireworks deep inside her. He brought her closer still, sliding his palm down her spine and continuing to kiss her in a way that was both protective and possessive, and a second, even more powerful wave started to surge.

Her spirits soaring, Allison reveled in their closeness. He tasted so good, like mint and man, desire and determination. He felt so good, too, so big and warm and athletically strong.

Aware he wanted her as much as she wanted him, she surrendered to the seductive pressure of his lips and buried her fingers in the thick strands of his hair. Knowing it wasn't physical need alone he was conjuring up, every time they made out like this, but a tidal wave of feelings, too.

She had missed him so much during the years they had been apart. Missed being able to let down her guard and lean on him.

Both for practical tasks, like help with the girls, and emotional things, too.

He had alleviated the loneliness she usually felt during the holiday season. And helped her deal with how much she wanted that new job.

Through it all, being sexy, steadfast and reliably tender in a way he never had been before.

As he continued to kiss and hold her close, she knew she was falling for him all over again.

And, more astonishing still, no longer sure she really minded.

Was it possible it could work out between them this time? If they kept things casual, their expectations low? Allison wasn't sure as their slow, sultry good-night kiss came to an end. All she really knew was that their babysitting stint would soon be over, and she did not want to let him go.

Chapter Thirteen

"It's awfully cheerful around here," Cade said the following morning when he walked in to see all smiles, and not a single pout!

Allison looked especially gorgeous, in a Christmas-plaid button-up flannel shirt he recalled from their college days. Instead of her usual tailored wool slacks or skirts, she had on snug-fitting dark denim jeans and fancy red cowgirl boots. She had put her hair up in a loose twist on the back of her head, and tendrils escaped to frame her flushed cheeks and the elegant nape of her neck.

"That's because we got up extra early and were extra busy this morning," Allison said.

Resisting the urge to haul her close and press a string of kisses up the slope of her throat, he said casually, "I noticed!"

Oblivious to the romantic nature of his thoughts, Jade and Sienna took him by the hand. "Come look at what we did!" they commanded, taking him over to the newly decorated "family tree" in the living room.

It was filled with handmade construction-paper chains, felt ornaments and pictures of all four girls from each previous Christmas. The lower branches also held plastic-wrapped candy canes.

"Mommy painted these while we were in her tummy!" Amber pointed to the wooden ornaments.

"And we helped her make these!" Hazel exclaimed, gesturing toward an array of colored Styrofoam balls with uneven glitter application.

"We wanted to put stickers on our tree," Sienna explained, "but Mommy said they wouldn't stick, so we put them on the Christmas tree skirt instead."

"Very nice," Cade complimented.

Allison joined them. She tucked her arm in his and slid her fingers around his bicep, reminding him how good it had felt when they'd been a couple. "I think so, too."

"Nobody has a tree like us," Jade said seriously.

Loving the feel of Allison snuggled against him, Cade wrapped his arm about her waist, bringing her closer still. "I would have to agree with you there."

Sienna left and came back with a plate holding

three blueberry pancakes. "Miss Allison saved these for you, Mr. Cade!"

Jade frowned. "But she wouldn't let us put syrup or butter on it yet because she said *you* had to do that."

Cade grinned appreciatively. "Very thoughtful."

Allison clapped her hands. "Okay, girls. It's almost time to leave for school, so everybody go upstairs and comb your hair and brush your teeth."

"Okay!" They scampered off.

"Wow." Cade carried his breakfast into the kitchen. He slid the plate into the microwave to reheat. "What a great start to the day."

Zeus ambled in and curled up in the corner.

"I know." Allison knelt to pet him. She looked up, ecstatic. "Amazing, isn't it? Especially given how they felt about the tree we brought in initially." She eased graciously upright.

He watched her walk across the kitchen, taking in a brief but pleasurable glimpse of her slender waist and full breasts. "It's no wonder they didn't like your perfectly ordered tree if that—" Cade angled his head "—was actually what they were coveting." He took his plate and sat down at the island.

Allison handed him silverware, butter and syrup, then got the lunch bags out of the fridge. Mood turning abruptly sentimental, she raked her teeth over the luscious softness of her lower lip. "I guess I'd forgotten all the stuff my mom and I made that we

hung on our tree when I was growing up," she ru-
minated softly.

To his pleasure, the blueberry pancakes were as
delicious as they looked. "Do you still have any of
it?" he asked curiously.

Allison frowned at the sudden sounds of rough-
housing on the second floor. "I think so. I'll have to
look." She strode to the stairs and called up, "Girls,
stay on task!"

"Okay, Miss Allison!" they shouted back.

Wild giggles followed.

Cade put his dishes in the dishwasher, aware all
over again what a good mother she would make one
day. "What do you think they're up to?" Clearly, she
had some idea.

She tilted her head and the gentle movement brought
the subtle drift of her perfume. "I think they were going
to try to make their hair look funny this morning. At
least that's what they were whispering about when they
were decorating the tree."

"Let me guess." He mugged comically. "They
think you don't know."

Rolling her eyes, she explained wryly, "I'm a
grown-up. And a mommy stand-in, to boot. Therefore clueless."

The moment drew out, making them feel more
like parents than ever. Even though their stint as the
babysitters for the quadruplets was nearing an end.

Seeming to realize that, too, she stiffened in a way

that made him wonder if she were going to miss the special moments like this as much as he was.

There was no clue in her dark green eyes. She cleared her throat and continued cheerfully, "Speaking of grown-up things... Are you ready for the interview this morning?" She bent over to put the syrup and the butter back in the fridge. It was a nice view. A *very* nice view.

Cade tried not to think about the scrutiny to come. "Yep," he said, figuring he would either get the job or he wouldn't. Worrying wouldn't change anything. "What about you?" Noticing some of the breakfast-table chairs were askew, he set them right. They were sticky, too. "Did you get any more tasks in?" He went to get a paper towel and the spray cleaner.

Allison nodded and busied herself wiping down the counters. "They want to see two more blog posts in the next twenty-four hours. The first, a light holiday meal prepped at home. The next, a Dos and Don'ts for Holiday Decorating."

Finished, Cade tossed the paper towel into the trash. She did the same. "They're really upping the pressure," he noted, looking down at her.

Her usual confidence shone through. "Not to worry. I've already got a few ideas for both. I just have to go home and get started."

The girls came running down the stairs in tandem, their hair thoroughly moussed and sticking out all over. Looking at them, Cade and Allison couldn't help but laugh.

"Take our picture so we can send it to Mommy and Daddy!" Amber demanded.

"Yeah," Hazel joked, doing first cartwheels and then somersaults across the living room, "tell them we're all ready to go to school!" She dropped to the floor and propped her legs in the air, bicycling away.

Allison took it all in stride. "Okay," she said, "but then we really have to finish getting ready and get to school…"

"You know I've got this," Allison said, minutes later as she escorted the girls out to Sarabeth's Suburban. "If you need to go…"

Cade knew they only had a few more days left jointly caring for the kids. He didn't want to miss a minute of it. "No, I have time," he said.

Drop-off went smoothly. Aware how familiar and right this all felt, Cade drove back to the house where both their vehicles were parked. Allison's in the driveway, his at the curb.

She touched his arm as he was turning off the ignition. "Hey," she said softly, her eyes going all serious. She drew a deep, bolstering breath. "Good luck today."

"Thanks," he replied, glad she was on his side. He had missed her love and support.

She leaned over to kiss him sweetly, tenderly. He

gathered her close and deepened the kiss. His body surged to life. "Good thing I have somewhere to be," he said gruffly. "Otherwise…"

She laughed softly. "Same here, slugger. Same here…"

Cade left reluctantly and headed for the Laramie County School District administration building. It was early, but the superintendent, athletic director and school board members were already there.

Everyone was serious, and they got right down to business.

"We'd love to have someone of your talent and experience, but we have to know—" the superintendent was stern "—are we going to be able to trust you with our kids? And know that you're making the right decisions for them and their futures? That you don't just want to play—and win—at all costs…?"

That attitude, Cade knew, was what had caused the loss of his relationship with Allison. He wasn't going to repeat it again. Nor would he sugarcoat the reality of the sports world. So he told the assembled group the truth. And fielded a grueling series of questions from them for the next three hours. Some of which were fair. Some of which, well, he didn't think they had a right to know. He answered them all anyway.

When the inquiry was finally over, he went down the line, shaking hands with everyone in the room.

CATHY GILLEN THACKER   215

"When will you decide whether or not I've got the job?" he asked before heading out the door.

"Early next week," the superintendent said.

He nodded, feeling emotionally wrung out and physically all wound up. "Fair enough."

He called Allison the moment he climbed into his pickup truck. "Had lunch yet?"

"No." Her voice was soft, curious.

"Want to go out?" he asked gruffly, hoping she wasn't too busy with work to see him.

To his relief, she didn't even hesitate. "Why don't you come here?"

Relief coursed through him. "Be right there."

Ten minutes later, he was walking in. Allison's dark brown hair had been brushed into a sleek shoulder-length bob and she was dressed in what he had come to think of as her work clothes. Today, it was a pretty cranberry dress with three-quarter-length sleeves. The knit fabric clung to her supple curves. Matching pumps set off her spectacular legs.

A beautiful salad was perfectly staged on the center of the dining table. Her camera and video recorder were both nearby. The table was set for one. "Am I interrupting?"

She shook her head, looking as glad to see him as he was to be there. "I just finished the first blog posting," she said.

Which had been something about a meal for one, he remembered.

"But not to worry. There's plenty to share."

He could see that. He took off his sport coat, loosened his tie and rolled up his sleeves. "A perk of the job, I guess."

She smiled at him. "Sometimes." She handed him another place setting and then went back to pour two iced teas.

He put his plate opposite hers. "Does it ever feel too much?"

She breezed back. Their fingers brushed as she gave him his beverage. They clinked glasses in a silent toast. "First, I normally set my own schedule. So I'm in total control of the workload." She sipped. "Second, I try to stay ahead of the postings. That way if I have a day where I can't get something finished, I still have something new to put up for the readers."

He grinned. "You've always had a gift for making things work, no matter the hardship."

"Except us." She clapped a hand over her lips the second the words were out. "I'm sorry." Clearly aggravated with herself, she averted her eyes and shook her head. "I don't know why I said that."

"I do." They needed to talk about this. He waited until she returned her gaze to his. "Maybe we didn't try hard enough…"

A long moment passed as she considered that. Finally, she released a long, uneven breath. "And maybe that was the way it was meant to be, at least then."

Maybe. But now, he vowed, would be different.

She smiled and pushed on, directing the conversation to what he'd really come there to talk about. "How did your job interview go?"

He helped her with her chair, her kindness a balm to his soul. "Not as well as I'd hoped."

She served him a generous helping of field greens, topped with crisp apple wedges, toasted pecans, cranberries and luscious slices of grilled chicken. "Why not?" she asked, indignant, handing over a crystal decanter of homemade poppy seed salad dressing.

He added a light amount, then watched as she did the same. "They've heard the rumors that I lied about my recovery so I could pitch in the playoffs."

Her delicate brows knit. "But you saw an orthopedist recommended by someone on the Wranglers management team! You were cleared to play. Medically, as far as the second injury went, it was a situation that could have gone either way."

It felt good to have her defending him. "I know. And I told them that," he retorted gently.

Allison picked up her fork. "But…?"

"They don't want to see any of the kids in the district being encouraged to make a similar wrong decision."

"You would never do that."

He liked it when they talked like this. It made him feel closer to her. "You're right," he confided, matter-of-fact. "I *don't* want to see anyone else endure a career-ending injury."

"Do the people interviewing you for the position understand that?"

"I hope so." Cade wasn't surprised to find the salad tasted as perfect as it looked. "I really want the challenge of figuring out the best way to work with and inspire kids. The way I was inspired, early on. Especially when I was a foster kid."

Allison regarded him curiously. "What do you mean? Did you have a special coach?"

Cade nodded. "Coach Randy. He was barely out of college. A volunteer at the local boys club. He didn't have a lot of innate athletic talent himself. Not like some of the coaches I had later on. But he threw me a lifeline. Helped me see that even though I had lost my folks, and was having a really hard time in foster care, that I could still play ball and be part of a team. Practice. Get better. He taught me to look on the bright side. That hard work and discipline do pay off."

"Well, you certainly have those traits in spades."

Cade warmed at her praise. "Now all I have to do is figure out how to pass them on…"

"Well, that should be easy." Her lips took on a determined slant. "All you have to do is be yourself."

Aware she was beginning to get a little too worked up on his behalf, which was something he certainly hadn't intended, he reached over and took her hand in his. Appreciating how pretty and sexy she looked in the soft afternoon light, as well as how much he wanted to make love to her, he teased, "Flattery will get you everywhere, Miss Allison." At least every-where he wanted them to go.

"It's not flattery," Allison huffed, oblivious to how much he wanted her in bed, beneath him. "You're really good with people, Cade! You love baseball. And you know the beauty and the ugliness of the sports world." She twined her fingers more inti-mately with his. "Who better to guide the kids who think they may want that as a way of life?"

Cade's body hardened. "I should have taken you with me. You could have acted as my agent."

She sat back abruptly, squaring her shoulders in a way that lifted, then lowered the luscious curves of her breasts. Vibrant pink color flooded her cheeks. "High school coaches don't have agents!"

"What about hot dates?" He gazed into her fiery green eyes, loving her passionate nature. He goaded her facetiously, "Are we allowed to have those?"

Mischief piqued her expression. "It depends," she teased him right back. She let her gaze drift over him slowly. As if mentally undressing him. "Are you speaking literally or figuratively?"

His blood pulsed all the hotter. "Both. So what do you say?" he asked, keeping his eyes locked with hers. "Will you go out with me when our babysitting gig is up?"

Part of Allison had been waiting for Cade to sig-nal he wanted more out of their resurging relationship than occasional heart-to-hearts and convenient lovemaking. Actually going on a date would be a definite Next Step. Yet it wasn't a request without complications, which made it a hard question to answer. "You mean in public?" she asked, buying time to formulate a response that wouldn't get her in hot water.

He nudged her knee under the table, sending a shiver of awareness running through her. "Well, we could skulk around in hats, sunglasses and trench coats, but I think that would draw a lot of attention, too."

She met his gaze. "Funny."

His eyes darkened seriously. "You didn't answer my question." He nudged her knee again.

Another shiver of awareness ran through her. "Can I think about it?"

He frowned, seeming to think she shouldn't need to consider the pros and cons. "Your brand?"

Why pretend it was anything else? If she owed him anything, it was complete honesty. And she wanted him to be candid in return. "I've got a lot riding on the way things play out over the next few weeks."

He paused, his expression turning as thoughtful as his low tone. "I guess we both do."

Finished, he rose and helped her clear the table. As he moved, he caught sight of a plastic storage box sitting next to her previously decorated "single woman" Christmas tree. The lid was off. Poorly crafted decorations, similar to the ones the quadruplets had put on their own tree that morning, were in plain view.

Allison winced in embarrassment. She had meant to put that away before anyone else saw it.

"What's all this?" he asked, moving toward it.

Wishing she didn't suddenly feel so vulnerable, she quipped, "A half-traveled wrong road."

He touched an ornament that said *Merry Christmas to Mommy!* across the front in white paint. On the back was a crookedly drawn heart and *Love, Allison, 3rd grade.* Seeing it that morning had brought Allison to tears. Something else she was glad Cade had not witnessed.

Studying it, Cade appeared touched. "Did you make this?" he asked gently.

Allison remembered the day she had given it to her mother. How happy her mom had been. Her throat tightened. "Yes. As well as a lot of the other things in the box."

Cade studied the handmade treasures with a sentimentality she hadn't expected. "I've never seen them," he marveled, casting her a curious look. "Even when we were dating."

With good reason, Allison thought. "I was a teenager by then." She flushed in embarrassment. "My mom wanted to put them up, but I thought it was way too cheesy, so my mom put it all away in this box. She told me one day it would mean a lot more than I could imagine. She was right." More so than Allison could have ever dreamed.

Cade turned to take her in his arms. "The kids inspired you to get this out?"

Not the way he thought. Although that was kind of the way it had turned out when she had actually been confronted with the deeply sentimental items.

Taking a deep breath, Allison eased away from him and the enticing comfort he offered. Still feeling a little off-kilter, she admitted, "I was going to use it in my Dos and Don'ts post."

He lifted a brow.

Appreciating how ruggedly handsome he looked, she continued explaining, "Take the original photos of my elegantly decorated tree, then add all the memorabilia and point out that we all outgrow the sentimentality of our youthful artwork at some point." She waved an airy hand at the half-finished project. "And that these kinds of things really shouldn't be seen. But then I began to wonder if it's ever really too late for a walk down memory lane." She shrugged, pushing away the heartache she'd felt over missing her mother and the Christmases they'd had, while simultaneously yearning to build something substantial with Cade. At least for this holiday season. "I mean, what are the rules, anyway?" she pushed on uncertainly.

He drew her against him and stroked a hand through her hair. Then pressed a light, comforting kiss on her temple. "I don't know that there have to be any when it comes to decorating for Christmas."

"Exactly." She leaned her head on his chest, the intimacy of the moment prompting her to admit thickly, unshed tears burning her eyes once again, "But I do know this. Seeing those ornaments again… along with taking care of the girls with you this last week…has made me realize how much I miss my mom and the closeness we shared. And not having family of my own makes the holidays especially hard," she rasped. Harder than she had been willing to admit to herself.

He looked down at her adoringly. "You have to realize I'm only a request away…"

She drew a breath and tried to get a grip on her soaring emotions. This was all due to the upheaval in their lives, the Christmas season and the bittersweet nostalgia of what might have been, she promised herself. Nothing more. But as his head came down and his lips slanted across hers, it was hard not to feel completely, wonderfully overwhelmed.

His kiss was everything she wanted. Teasing and tempting. Provocative and lush. Tender and sexy. She rose on tiptoe and pressed her breasts against the hardness of his chest. He cradled her against him. Eyes smoldering, he lifted her legs and wrapped them about his waist. Then, still kissing her, he began carrying her up the stairs to the second floor.

"We're really doing this again," she murmured breathlessly, as he set her down beside her bed.

"We really are."

Desire floated through her, whisper soft. "Well, merry Christmas to both of us," she said.

He laughed. "Merry Christmas, indeed." Smiling wickedly, he caught her lower lip between his teeth, drew it into his mouth and laved it sensually with his tongue.

She shuddered at the evocative feel of his heated caress and closed her eyes. He made her feel so alive. So...his. She moaned, savoring everything about him. His hardness. His strength. The sheer masculinity that permeated everything about him as they began to kiss and caress each other. And kiss some more...

"Too slow," she complained.

"Slow can be nice." He kissed his way down the nape of her neck, then turned her so her back was to him. And eased open the zipper on her dress. She shuddered in anticipation as he drew it down her arms and pushed it over her hips.

Clad in panties and bra, she turned to face him. Shifted her hips. Encountering rock-solid hardness, searing heat.

She quivered as his hands found the clasp of her bra and drew that off, too. "I think we're on the right path." His hands found her breasts. He palmed the weight of them, stroking her nipples with his thumbs, generating raw, aching need. And though Allison had told herself this could be nothing more than a holiday fling, something fun and distracting to get them through the season, she knew, if she were completely honest with herself, that wasn't true. She wanted so much more from their relationship.

She wanted to know that she could count on Cade to be there whenever she needed him. That if they were together again, this time it wouldn't be all about his career, but hers, too. She wanted him to be as patient with her as she had once been with him. To mean the world to each other. And as she swayed against him wantonly and opened her mouth to the plundering heat of his, as he eased her panties off, too, she began to think that maybe this Christmas, all her dreams might finally come true...

Cade hadn't known when he and Allison would make love again. But he *had* known it was just a matter of time. After all, there was simply no way they could spend this much time together and stay apart.

And now that she was in his arms again, surging against him, trembling with need, he was all in.

Not just for the sex. Although that was, as always, fantastic. But for her intuition and her kindness, her understanding and even her sass.

She got him. She always had. And he knew her, too.

Knew she liked it when he guided her down onto the bed and held her gaze deliberately when he stripped down to join her. Knew her heart beat just for him when she opened her arms, rolled onto her side and brought him against her, kissing him hungrily until they were both groaning for more.

A rush of need surged through him, and the frustration and yearning he'd been feeling all day finally began to ease.

For weeks now, since his last injury, he hadn't known where he belonged. Or with whom.

Now he did.

And soon Allison would know, too.

Big hands encircling her hips, he shifted her so one leg was drawn over his hip, the other caught between his knees. His hand slid over her limbs, stroking the tender insides of her thighs, finding the pleasure point as even more passionate kisses were exchanged.

She found him, too. Running her soft hands over the ridge of his erection. Stroking and tempting until he could hardly wait to be inside her again.

"Now?" he growled.

She smiled, shuddering with anticipation. "Now…"

He let her go long enough to find the protection they needed. She surrendered completely, opening herself up to him as she wrapped her arms and legs around him. He slid home. And suddenly there was no more waiting, no more wondering, only the pleasure and the bliss, the fire and the passion of their joining. They made love as if nothing else in the world mattered, and for a while, nothing else did.

Chapter Fourteen

"So, what's the plan for the rest of the day?" Cade murmured, kissing her one last time when they had finished dressing and walked back downstairs.

Allison knew the last thing she should have been doing that afternoon was snuggling in bed with Cade, but with her heart full and her body still humming with post-lovemaking satisfaction, she hadn't been any more eager to end their sensual interlude than he had been. And now, with school pickup time fast approaching, she was uncharacteristically disorganized. Yet she couldn't say she regretted any of it. Since he had come back into her life, and the two of them had started taking care of the quadruplets, her world felt more complete than it had in years.

"If you need to work more this afternoon, I can pick up the girls on my own," Cade continued.

Allison knew that was true. She also realized their time together as a temporary family was dwindling. And she didn't want to miss any of it.

Even if it meant leaving her "single woman" Christmas tree, half covered with sentimental items she had never intended to leave on for more than a few minutes, just as it was.

Easing out of his arms, she put the lid on the storage box and set it beneath the tree, figuring she'd remove the aforementioned items later when she had time. Then went back to gather up her workbag, laptop, cell phone and keys, aware how off-brand her life was beginning to feel. "I'll finish up my Dos and Don'ts post for HITN later this evening, after the girls are asleep."

"Okay, if you're sure…"

Allison took in the faint growth of beard and the flush of happiness on his rugged, chiseled face. It seemed impossible he could appear even sexier than he had when he'd been making love to her, but he did. "I am." She resisted the urge to pull him into her arms again and kiss him wantonly. "The girls were up so early this morning they're probably going to be really overtired."

He nodded in understanding and flashed her a lopsided smile. "And therefore, a handful."

An understatement, as it turned out.

Amber cried after school because she was convinced that Zeus missed Mommy and Daddy as much as they did. Jade became frustrated during their after-school coloring session, because no one else was putting as much effort into their pictures as she was. During dinner, Sienna insisted on assembling her own grilled chicken sandwich, then burst into tears when the excessive amount of mayo she'd slathered on caused the fillet to slide right out and land beside her plate. And through it all, Hazel was exceptionally silly and unable to settle down, and kept falling off her chair only to do acrobatics across the floor.

"When are Mommy and Daddy going to call us?" Amber demanded on a fresh wave of tears.

Hoping that might help, Allison met Cade's concerned look and said, "I'll text and find out."

The girls got up extra early and are in meltdown, Allison typed. Any chance you can FaceTime soon to calm them down?

A minute later, her phone rang. Allison set it up so all four girls could see. With Cade occasionally acting as referee, they all four took turns talking to their parents.

Finally, Sarabeth said, in a tone laced with maternal concern, "I'd like to talk to Allison alone a minute and go over a few things."

"Sure." She took the phone upstairs to start laying out pajamas.

"I just wanted to tell you that we haven't forgotten. We still plan to FaceTime with the girls Thursday right after school. So we can tell them ourselves we won't be at their holiday performance."

Allison could see that Sarabeth was still really disappointed about that, too. "Do you think that will be enough time for them to come to terms with the situation?" she asked, a little worried, given how moody and oft uncooperative the girls had already been.

Sarabeth frowned. "I don't know. I think it's the best we can do right now, though, so…"

Allison nodded and sat down on the edge of the bed. "You're the mom, so you know best."

Sarabeth's expression sparkled with mischief. "How are things going with you and Cade?"

Allison tried not to blush. "Um…good," she said casually.

The other woman's eyes narrowed. "Are you getting back together?"

"You know what?" She stood. "I think I hear him calling for me," Allison fibbed, feeling like their *reconciliation* was too new and fragile to be held up to outside scrutiny.

"We'll FaceTime again Thursday, then," Sarabeth promised.

They ended the call.

"What did Sarabeth want to talk to you about?" Cade asked later after the girls were in bed, asleep.

"The pre-K Christmas show." The dishes done, Allison brought out the makings for the next day's school lunches. She explained Sarabeth and Shawn were still planning to FaceTime with the quadruplets right after school on Thursday. "I'm worried about how the girls are going to handle their parents' absence."

He got out the sandwich bags. "Think they're going to act out?"

Allison laid out eight slices of bread on the cutting board. She layered slices of cheese on the bottom four while Cade added ham and then their favorite raspberry jam to the others.

"Well, obviously." Allison tried not to imagine the possible scenarios, all of them temperamental and overwrought. Together, they cut the sandwiches into triangle-shaped quarters and bagged them. Then slid them into the fridge until morning.

Allison turned to Cade, her back against the fridge. Once again, leaning on his solid, practical nature, she gazed into his eyes. "The real question is, will we be able to get them to calm down before the performance?"

He shrugged his broad shoulders, as if it were

no big deal. "Of course we will," he said, hugging her close.

Basking in his confidence, Allison breathed a sigh of relief. Cade was right. If anyone could charm them into behaving, it was him.

Except, as it turned out, it wasn't as easy as they had hoped. Especially since the girls' parents weren't the ones to break the news, after all.

"I am *so sorry*." Their pre-K teacher came out to the car to speak to them during afternoon pickup on Thursday. "I had no idea the quadruplets did not know their parents weren't going to be at the performance tonight. I tried to console them that the school was making a video that Shawn and Sarabeth would be able to watch when they returned from Switzerland."

Allison caught sight of the quadruplets' stormy expressions as they walked with the two mom volunteers to the Suburban. Easily able to see how upset they were, she tensed. "It's all right. We'll handle it," she said.

His gaze narrowing protectively, Cade reached over and squeezed Allison's hand. "Maybe we should stop by the bakery to get some bite-sized cupcakes to take to the after-show reception…and a few more to try out…before we head home?"

Appreciating how good he was at changing mess

into magic, Allison nodded in relief and squeezed his hand back. "Great idea," she said.

The girls did not think so.

They frowned at the amazing selection and adamantly refused to take sample bites of any of the delicious-looking treats, even after they got the girls home and offered them again.

Four lower lips shot out in petulant scowls. "Mommy has to come to our performance!" Jade declared.

Amber put both arms around Zeus's neck and hugged the family pet close. "Sometimes Daddy isn't there, and he doesn't get to see us, 'cause he is traveling, but Mommy *always* is!"

Hazel kicked the wall repeatedly with the toe of her sneaker. "They need to come back home!"

"Right now!" Sienna agreed.

Cade was already texting a message on his phone.

A minute later, Sarabeth and Shawn requested a video chat. Over the next ten minutes, they tried their best, but nothing they said wiped the glum looks off their children's faces.

"Allison and I are going to take a video, too," Cade soothed when the call had ended. "So we will all be able to look at it later," he finished, his low, sexy voice generating a tsunami of need deep within her.

Not daring to look him in the eye, Allison picked up where he had left off, instructing, "In the meantime, we need to eat an early dinner and then go upstairs and begin getting ready." The girls were due to arrive back at the school by 6:15 p.m., with the performance starting at 7:00 p.m.

Unfortunately, they didn't want their grilled cheese bites and apple slices any more than they had wanted to taste the sweet treats.

The process of getting ready went even worse. "I don't want my hair brushed!" Sienna shouted.

"These shoes hurt!" Hazel said.

"They won't stay on! They keep falling off!" Sienna agreed.

"I don't want to wear all the same dresses!" Jade said.

"And I'm not going unless Zeus can go with us!" Amber pouted.

Cade let out a whistle worthy of any athletic coach. The shrill sound stopped everyone in their tracks. "Enough," he said sternly, commanding the room as easily as he commanded a baseball field. He paused to look each one of the girls in the eye. "I know you're upset. I'm sorry about that. But we are going to go tonight. And we are going to have a good time, because that is what your mommy and daddy want us to do." He paused to let his words sink in while Allison breathed a silent sigh of relief. "Got it?"

The girls nodded glumly but did not argue further. While Allison rushed to get ready to go, too, and Cade took Zeus outside, the girls huddled on the sofa, pouting and talking softly among themselves.

Luckily, by the time they were out the door and on their way, the girls seemed to have come to the conclusion that whether their parents were present or not, the show was absolutely going to go on.

Parents and other family weren't allowed backstage, so Allison and Cade dropped the quadruplets off with their teacher and then took their seats. The performance wasn't going to start for another twenty minutes, yet Allison's pulse was racing. Cade struggled to fit his big tall body into the too-small seat and smiled over at her.

Where their knees and shoulders aligned, they also touched. "Excited?"

Aware all over again how warm and strong his body felt when pressed against hers, Allison nodded. "Yes," she said, smiling over at him. She couldn't say why exactly, but she sensed this was going to be a night they remembered. Partly because in getting the girls here tonight, they'd had a hand in it. And partly because, she acknowledged wistfully to herself, had she and Cade not broken up eight years prior, they would have taken a very different path. And in fact, could have very well had their own children in this celebration, too.

But they hadn't, so...the only thing that was left between them was the electric chemistry and kindhearted friendship they shared now.

Abruptly wondering if that was going to be enough,

for either of them, Allison noted how handsome he looked in his sport coat and tie. How ready to be a father, too.

And if that was true, too. Was it possible? Could they build on what they had now? Dare to pursue more?

Maybe the real question was, how could they not?

Swallowing around the sudden knot of emotion in her throat, she struggled to get her thoughts back on track. "What about you?" she asked, turning toward him slightly and feeling her knee nudge his thigh through the fabric of his slacks. "Are you excited?"

He squeezed her forearm affectionately. "Surprisingly so."

Not surprised to find them similarly affected, Allison waved at old friends who were coming into the other side of the auditorium, then turned back to Cade and leaned in close. "Thanks for being with me earlier. I don't think I could have managed that on my own tonight."

In an effort to get more comfortable in the too-small space, Cade rested his arm along the back of her chair. He tilted his head toward hers and squeezed her shoulder lightly. "Sure you could have," he countered easily. "But you're right. We are much better as a team."

He was right about that. Individually, they might make good stand-in parents. But together, they made great ones.

So, if family and Cade was what she wanted…and

she was beginning to see it was…why was she still holding back? Especially in this season of giving. No one had ever made her feel as happy and complete as Cade did. Yes, he could still hurt and disappoint her, and she could do the same to him. But she could also trust that they were older and wiser and would do much better this time, as a couple. And honestly, wasn't faith and hope what Christmastime was all about?

Ready finally to take the next step toward a happily-ever-after with him, she looked him in the eye. "You asked me about a hot date when our babysitting gig is all done," she reminded him in a soft, confidential tone. And she had delayed giving him a decision. No longer. "My answer is yes."

His grin widened, but he did not look surprised. He squeezed her shoulder again, promising, "I'll start planning for a night out, just the two of us, as soon as Shawn and Sarabeth get back to Laramie."

And knowing him, Allison suspected it would be *spectacular*.

More people filtered in. Near the stage on the other side of the room, his old baseball coach took a seat. His brother Gabe and his wife, Susannah, were also in attendance, to see their quintuplets perform, too. Cade nodded at them both when they waved. "Mind if I say hello?" he asked.

"Not at all." It would give her a chance to check

her messages. Which was something she hadn't had an opportunity to do.

As she'd half feared, there were several from Laurel Grimes. The last said, Call me ASAP!

Happy that Cade was otherwise occupied talking to family and old friends, she left her sweater on one seat, her bag on the other, marking them as taken, and then took her phone out into the far end of the hallway for privacy.

"Thank goodness!" the HITN producer said. "I've been trying to get you all afternoon."

Embarrassed to have been caught neglecting her work, in favor of her personal life, Allison murmured, "Sorry. What's up?"

"Tripp Taylor…"

The HITN programming director.

"…saw the salad post you put up. He had the same question I did. Why so much food? No single woman would eat that much in one sitting. And if your plan was to make enough for *two* meals, why didn't you show how to store the rest separately?"

Allison winced. "I…" The truth was, she had no reason. Other than her thoughts had also been on Cade and his interview, and how he might be feeling afterward, instead of just on her assigned task.

"Do you realize how tight this race is? You can't afford to be off-brand like that!"

Allison rubbed at the new tension in her temples. "I'll make sure it doesn't happen again."

"Good, because Jennifer Moore is doing everything perfectly. You still have a slight edge, thanks to the Dos and Don'ts holiday decorating advice you put up. Tripp Taylor thinks your blog is more relatable to the average viewer, and that the upscale audience *City Lights* targets might be more drawn to Gwyneth Paltrow's *Goop Lab* on Netflix than anything on HITN. But…if you slip up again, in any way…or fail to live up to your brand…"

Allison's whole body tensed. "I get it. I'll do better," she said, feeling a little panicky. Why had she convinced herself she could spend equal amounts of time on her personal life and her career, and still be just as successful?

Laurel warned, "Whatever you turn in tomorrow for the Scents of the Holiday post needs to be fabulous."

"It will be," Allison promised.

Aware the performance was about to start, she ended the call and headed back to find her seat. Cade scrutinized her. "Everything okay?"

She nodded. "Small problem at work. Nothing to worry about." Because she was going to fix it. Even if it meant staying up all night to do so.

The music started.

Slowly, the curtains parted.

The stage was filled with thirty pre-K students arranged in a single line, facing the audience. The quadruplets were all standing together toward the center of the group.

And Allison realized with a sinking heart that despite the way they had seemed to calm down after Cade's "pep talk," they still had not really regained their holiday spirit. As they sang "Deck the Halls," all four seemed to be scanning the audience, looking for their parents. They scowled as their gazes fell on Allison and Cade, and they continued looking as the first song ended and "Jingle Bells" began.

The audience oohed and aahed as the kids used handheld jingle bells to accentuate every note, giving the song an extra holiday feel.

Everyone, it seemed, but Sienna, who was wiggling her foot around in her sparkly too-stiff new shoes. Then, frowning, she toed one off.

Amber noticed and stopped singing long enough to give her sister a goading look.

Which compelled Sienna to toe off the other one, with even more force this time.

It flipped upward, went airborne, then sailed over the edge of the stage onto the floor. Fortunately, the combination of vigorously shaken jingle bells, the children's voices and the piano music muffled the splat of leather hitting tile. In fact, Allison noted with relief, most parents were so focused on their own kids that no one in the audience save Cade and herself really noticed. But Jade had seen, and she could not stop giggling. As "Silver Bells" started, she put both hands on her hips and easily kicked her own shoes off. They sailed out into the audience, causing several parents to chuckle, others to gasp in surprise and several more to frown.

"Oh, no," Allison whispered, clasping Cade's arm in horror.

"'Oh, no' is right," he murmured back, trying in vain to signal the girls to behave.

One of the "stage help" moms tried to get the attention of the girls from the wings, also with no luck. A grinning Hazel, no longer interested in the Christmas show at all, had decided to sit down, right where she was, and then do her favorite bicycling trick, with her hands holding up her hips, her skirt around her waist and her white-tight-clad legs pedaling hard and fast and high in the air.

Amber stepped closer to Hazel and began dancing ballerina-style around her as "Silver Bells" came to an end.

Worse, other students were seeing the quadruplets wildly misbehaving and were now off task, too, in the way only extremely excited four-year-olds could be. And just like that, it was like something out of the scene from *A Charlie Brown Christmas* where the play rehearsal abruptly spins out of control, and everyone was dancing and singing to their own tune.

The pianist started playing "Linus and Lucy," the music from that scene.

Amber went from pirouetting to rocking out.

Hazel stopped bicycling and shot to her feet, grinning. Jade and Sienna joined in, too. And that was all it took. Without exception, all the kids began mimicking variations of the Snoopy and Linus and Lucy choreography.

The parents, thinking it was a planned part of the performance, oohed and aahed in delight until the song ended and the curtains were closed.

Midshow!

"Should we go back?" Allison whispered, upset. Surely, they wouldn't end the program on account of the quadruplets when only half the slated songs had been performed!

Cade shook his head. He reached over to put his hand on her forearm, his warm, solid strength transmitting through her cardigan to her skin. "Let the teachers handle it."

Reluctantly, Allison did.

A very brief unplanned intermission was held. Finally, the drapes opened again and the performance continued, this time without interruption. Thunderous applause followed the last song. Feeling responsible for the melee, Allison and Cade went to collect the kids and take them to the cafeteria for the reception.

Seeing them, Gabe teased, "Well, you two babysitters clearly have everything under control."

Susannah, who'd had her own embarrassing moments with their quintuplets, elbowed her husband.

"Hush. Hi, Allison. I hear you're up for a big new job."

Allison blushed. She hadn't told anyone in Laramie about the HITN opportunity, so this had to have come from Cade. "It's just a possibility," she allowed, not wanting to jinx it.

Sobering, Gabe asked Cade, "Speaking of new jobs… Have you heard anything yet?"

Cade shook his head, his expression solemn. "Maybe by Monday. At least that's my hope."

Gabe clapped him on the back. "Good luck, bro."

He smiled. "Thanks."

"You really want it, don't you?" Allison murmured, while they threaded their way toward the kids, who were with the rest of their classmates, standing in line for treats.

Cade briefly wrapped his arm about her waist. "I need to go back to who I really am. A small-town guy with a big family, who grew up loving baseball."

Which begged the question, Allison thought, as she leaned into his warm, compelling touch. Who was she really? A blogger destined for fame? Or a small-town gal who was tired of being alone? And most important of all, wanted what Cade had with the big, loving Lockhart clan.

The girls were so exhausted by the time they got them home, it was all Allison could do to get them into their pj's, while Cade helped them brush their teeth. Together, they tucked them in.

Their eyes shut as soon as the lights were out. Five minutes later, all were sound asleep.

"I know you planned to work this evening," Cade mentioned, as he walked downstairs with her.

She thought about what Laurel Grimes had said. How unhappy she had been with Allison, and how unhappy Allison had been with herself. Figuring Cade didn't need to know that she had been more concerned with being there for him than properly fine-tuning her latest work challenges, she forced herself to get her ambition back on track. "Yes. I do."

To her relief, he understood completely. He tucked an errant strand of her hair behind her ear. "How can I help?"

She watched Zeus rise and amble toward the front door, where he sat, waiting to go out. "Take Zeus for one last walk for me and then head home, so I can proceed without distraction?"

He eased her beneath the mistletoe the quadruplets had insisted on putting up. Seeming not to mind at all that she was kicking him out, he kissed her tenderly. "I think I can handle that."

Allison wreathed her arms about his neck. "I'm happy to hear that," she teased in return, aware all over again how very glad she was to have him back in her life. Even if she was going to have to be careful to keep things in balance professionally, after they started casually dating. And not let her love life upend her career goals, or her overly romantic notions cause her to misrepresent the facts to herself.

Yes, she and Cade had always made a good team when it came to being friends and lovers. It was when they let themselves expect more than that from each other, while they both navigated the career issues in their lives, that they'd hit a rough patch.

So, even if part of her still wanted marriage and a family with Cade, still wanted that dreamy happily-ever-after, there was another part of her that knew she could be content with things just as they were. And so could he.

At least through the holidays... Now, if she could just get the job she wanted, it would be a very merry Christmas, indeed.

Chapter Fifteen

"Are you sure you're not mad at us?" Amber asked the next morning before school.

Jade ate a spoonful of cereal. "So mad you have to leave?"

A hopeful expression on her face, Sienna played with her toast. "And Mommy and Daddy have to come back early?"

Allison looked at Cade as a light bulb went off in her head. So *that* was what all the chaos on stage had been about! The girls had developed what they'd clearly felt was a surefire plan and then executed it during the performance.

Cade met her eyes and grinned in rueful acknowledgment. Clearly, they'd been had! Sobering, she turned back to the girls. "Your parents will be home as soon as the doctors give your dad permission to fly," she promised.

In unison, the girls sighed, clearly disappointed their antics hadn't worked. "We miss Mommy and Daddy," the usually comical Hazel said glumly.

"I know," Allison said gently.

"We all do," Cade agreed.

The meal over, he stood and held out his arms. "Group hug."

The girls sighed again but slid out of their chairs and moved toward him. He beckoned Allison over their heads, and she moved in to join the huddle.

It was moments like these, she thought, that made her long for a family of her own. With Cade. Which in turn made her wonder if her perfect single-woman life was going to be sustainable.

Fortunately, duty called. And she didn't have any more time to think about it.

Together, she and Cade dropped the girls off at school.

He had just emerged from the car-pool line, onto the street, when Allison's phone dinged, signaling a FaceTime request from Sarabeth coming in. Worried how they would take what had ultimately happened, she said, "Here we go," and put her phone on speaker. The quadruplets' parents appeared on-screen. "Hi, Sarabeth. Shawn."

"Hey," Sarabeth said cheerfully. "How did the performance go last night?"

Allison turned the phone toward her companion. Cade waved and continued driving.

"Shawn and I are dying to hear," Sarabeth continued.

"Well, there were a few hijinks," Allison said slowly. And then she explained.

To her relief, the quadruplets' parents found it as amusing as most of the audience had. Especially when they understood the reason why, as had been revealed over breakfast. "Can we see it?" Shawn asked.

"Sure. Hang on." Allison paused to send the video, then went back to the call. "It's a little long, so it may take a few minutes to come through. In the meantime, how are your plans for return?" she asked.

"The doctors finally decided it's safe for Shawn to travel. So we managed to get a flight home first thing tomorrow morning. But there's a possibility of bad weather coming in that could delay our flight out of Switzerland, so we'd rather not tell the girls we're coming home until we actually make it as far as Dallas."

"That's probably a good idea."

Sarabeth grinned as her phone dinged. "The video just came in!"

"Enjoy it," Allison said, then let them go so they

could watch the very memorable performance they had missed.

Cade turned onto the street where he lived. Surprised, Allison asked, "Are we stopping by your house?"

"Do you mind?" he said. "I need to check on a couple of things."

"Do you want me to wait outside or come in?"

He sent her a droll look, then surveyed her head to toe, as if he found her completely irresistible. "Come in." He chuckled, a deep rumbling low in his throat.

Trying not to think how attracted she was to him, too, Allison wrinkled her nose. "Okay." Aware she hadn't been in his Laramie home yet, and curious… as a woman *and* as an interior designer…to see what he had done to the elegantly updated Craftsman, she followed him inside. It was every bit as opulent as everyone had said. With a pitched roof and expansive front porch, centered with a beautifully crafted front door with windows on either side, as well as above. Inside, the large foyer opened up into a great room with a state-of-the-art kitchen on one side, a cozy gathering space the other. Dark wide plank oak floors coordinated perfectly with heavy masculine furniture and jewel-toned area rugs. Through the picture windows that flanked the rear wall of the home, she could see the wooden privacy fence and the waterfall pool, now covered for winter, contained therein.

Cade turned to her. "What do you think?"

Finding his steady regard a little unnerving, Allison continued moving about the room. She paused to examine the big-screen TV hidden behind double doors above the mantel. "It's very masculine and luxurious." Very much the perfect bachelor lair. Just as her home was the ideal abode for a single woman whose sole focus was her career.

Apparently not realizing that those two facts alone should tell them something, he sauntered over to join her. "I think it needs a new design."

Allison pushed aside a feeling of déjà vu. "That's up to you."

"I think it's too Big-City Bachelor for Laramie."

True, but that was exactly what he had been when he'd been playing for the Wranglers and purchased the place. "What did you want it to be?"

He paused to look over at her, all indomitable male once again. "Small-town baseball coach."

And family man? Deciding she was getting way ahead of herself, she smiled. Then, attempting to keep the mood light and carefree between them, she said, "If you want me to give you some names…"

He ambled close enough to kiss her. Tunneled both hands through her hair and lifted her face to his. "I want you to do it," he said gruffly.

Splaying her hands across his chest, she inhaled his familiar cedarwood-and-rain scent. Afraid of progressing too far, too fast, she challenged, "Haven't we been down this road before?"

He lifted one of her hands and kissed the back of it, rubbing his lips erotically over her skin. "And what road is that?" he asked softly, still holding her gaze.

A tingle of awareness swept through her. Lingering, low. Yearning welling up inside of her, she swayed against him. "You don't have to hire me to design the interior of your home to spend time with me when our babysitting gig ends. We agreed to date, remember?"

He regarded her affectionately, looking sexy as all get-out with a day's worth of beard rimming his ruggedly handsome face. "What if I just want you to design the interior of my home?"

Telling herself this was not the time to indulge in unrealistic fantasies, Allison stepped back and replied in her most matter-of-fact tone, "I'd still suggest you think about having someone else do it." She perched on the back of the sofa.

He sat beside her and covered her hand with his. "How come?"

She looked down at their entwined fingers, aware how much she enjoyed being with him, no matter where they were or what they were doing. "I don't want to start something and not be able to finish it."

"I don't, either." Guiding her to her feet, he danced

her backward until she was standing on the edge of the foyer and the great room.

"If I get the TV show—" as she was very close to doing, especially with the work she had put in the previous night and posted very early this morning "—I'll be so busy I won't be able to finish this." She gestured around them.

He wrapped his arms around her and pulled her close until they were touching in one electric line. "You could, if you took your time." He pressed a kiss to the sensitive place behind her ear.

A whisper of desire swept through her, weakening her knees. "Cade…"

"Like I'm planning to do right now." He kissed her nose, her cheek.

Allison moaned. "I…"

"Look up," he commanded.

Curious, she did. "Mistletoe!" She laughed at the sight of it. Shook her head in wonderment. "So, you did get some after all!"

"Not just one sprig," he relayed as his mouth locked on hers in a slow, sexy caress that made her tingle from head to toe.

It was in the foyer. The hallway. His bedroom doorway. Even over his bed.

He kissed her beneath every single mistletoe. So warm and strong. So unbelievably tender and persistent in his pursuit of her. And she opened her heart in return. Wreathing her arms about his neck, shifting her body close. He tasted so good. So dark and male. And he felt even better. All warm, solid muscle. She could feel the hard evidence of his desire as he slid his hands down her body, cupping her against him. And still he kissed her, sweetly and irrevocably, possessing her heart and soul, until she thought she would melt from the pleasure of it.

The next thing she knew, they were stripping down. Exploring rapaciously. Tumbling together onto his bed. He shifted onto his back; she straddled his middle. Then, with his big, strong hands molding her breasts, kissing her ravenously again, he moved up, then in. Satisfaction flooded through every part of her. And finally, there was no more waiting. Or holding back. Her back arched, her body shuddering and coming apart, the passion she felt for him dissolving in wild carnal waves. She whispered his name... He called out to her in return. And then they both surrendered to a molten hot passion unlike anything she had ever known.

Afterward, they cuddled together, and she knew this was what it felt like when it was right, when love was about to happen. All over again. He lifted his head and gazed into her eyes. Regarded her quietly. "What are you thinking?" he asked, still holding her in a way that made her feel incredibly cherished and protected.

Joy rose inside her. Figuring she might as well admit it, she said, "That as much as I can't wait for

Sarabeth and Shawn to come home and be reunited with their girls, I am definitely going to miss *playing house* with you and the kids." This had been the first time in her life she'd had even an inkling what it would be like to really be part of a big, boisterous, loving family. And she had adored it.

"Hey." He brushed his lips reverently over hers. "We don't have to stop playing house just because we don't have to watch the girls..."

Her body still humming deliciously, she chided, "You know what I mean..."

"I do." Tunneling both hands through her hair, he kissed her again, with all the tenderness she had ever hoped to receive. "And I'm serious, Allison. I want you back in my life. Every day. And every way. From now on..."

"Oh, Cade, I want that, too." Her heart filling with deep, searing emotion, she blinked back tears of joy. As she kissed him back, she felt him begin to get aroused. As did she.

"Round two?" he teased.

"Why not?" she started to say. "We've got time..."

Her phone dinged to signal an incoming text. Cade groaned at the interruption, dropped his head down on the pillow and closed his eyes. "I know..." Allison said softly. "I don't want to look at it, either, but with all I am responsible for at the moment, I have to..."

She read the message once, her mouth going dry with apprehension. And then again.

Alarmed, Cade pushed to a sitting position. "What is it?" he asked.

Allison sat up, too. "The HITN execs are on their way to see me. They have a very serious matter they want to discuss with me in regard to the story that just broke on the *Personalities!* magazine website."

Cade got his laptop and brought it back to bed. Together, they looked up the *Personalities!* story that included photos of her and Cade. Waiting to see Santa at the mall. Driving the kids to school. Hugging—and kissing—on Sarabeth and Shawn's doorstep, as they said goodbye to each other at the end of the night. And the salacious print article was even more damning:

Rekindled Love?

Forced to retire, Wranglers pitcher Cade Lock-hart returned to his hometown of Laramie, Texas, hoping to begin a high school coach-ing career, and instead has found love again with his former sweetheart, up-and-coming lifestyle blogger Allison Meadows. That love could come at a cost, however, if she loses a potential TV-hosting gig because of the ro-mance. HITN isn't against marriage per se.

In fact, the other candidate for their proposed new lifestyle show geared for thirtysomethings, City Lights *blogger Jennifer Moore, is admittedly on the hunt for a fiancé. It's been Allison Meadows who was set to speak to other thirtysomethings who definitely don't want or need a love relationship in their lives to be content. In fact, that's what her popular blog,* My Cottage Life, *is all about. "I don't know who HITN is going to choose," Jennifer Moore said when asked to comment. "I just know they want whoever it is to be authentic."*

"Uh-oh," Cade said.

Her heart racing, Allison dashed out of bed and began to get dressed. She turned to see the distressed look on his face. Her heart sank. "What?"

"There's another story on the *Celebrity Grapevine* website." With a frown, he showed her the article.

Nothing but a Fraud?

My Cottage Life *blogger Allison Meadows has been writing about how great the holidays are for a single lady (see sidebar photos from her blog) while in actuality spending all her holiday time with four adorable little kids and her ex-love Cade Lockhart, a retired pro baseball player who has had his own problems with honesty. (He lied about his fitness to return to play, a move that cost the Wranglers their bid for the division championship.) Now, check out the photos from her real world. Doesn't look like the satisfied single life to us...!*

His expression turned unrelentingly grim as he and Allison studied the pictures.

The first was of Cade, in uniform, on the pitching mound, shortly before he suffered his final injury. Another of when he was being helped off the field. And later, one of Cade politely listening to the Wranglers-cap-wearing fan at the mall while Allison and the kids sat nearby.

But that was just the beginning...

There was a snapshot of Cade and Allison picking out a tree and buying mistletoe with the girls. Another of them all walking into the school together for the pre-K Christmas performance. Those were juxtaposed with her photos from her recent blog posts. Single-handedly decorating her cottage. Making meals for one. Putting up a "single woman" holiday tree.

It did look like it was all a lie, Allison realized miserably.

"It wasn't just an accident we ran into that man in the Wranglers cap at the mall, or that he had a woman with him, taking pictures that day, when he tried to start something with you," she said, thinking about the time she thought she had seen him outside the preschool, too. "He was following us, all along!"

Cade nodded in agreement. He got up and began to dress, too. "He may have even been hired to do it."

Allison bent to slip on her shoes. "By whom?"

Shrugging, Cade zipped his jeans and pulled on his shirt. "Jennifer Moore warned you that she was going to prove you weren't authentic."

Allison accompanied Cade down the stairs. "But how would she know I would fall for you?" she asked, upset.

"Maybe she didn't." Cade's glance narrowed. "Maybe she was just set on catching you in any kind of potentially controversial incident that would put you out of the running and leave the field wide open for her. The fact that you were babysitting the quadruplets at the time, and we rekindled our love affair again after I lent a helping hand, was just plain dumb luck."

Or inevitable. With effort, Allison forced herself back to the problem at hand. "Well, whatever the case, we can't let this misconception stand. We have to come up with an explanation HITN will accept."

"What do you mean?"

She folded her arms across her chest. "I can't publicly be part of a couple because that's not my brand."

He stared at her as if she were a complete stranger. "We're talking about your *career*?"

"Yes," Allison explained patiently, sure she could

make him see things her way. "I won't get my own television show with HITN unless we go to the executives, when they get here, and explain to them that this was all a misunderstanding."

His brow furrowed. "In what sense?" He stepped closer.

"Well...we'll just tell them that the pictures are misleading. And admit that while we once had a thing, explain that the fact it didn't work out was what propelled me to seek an independent life of my own for the last eight years. And even though we recently spent a lot of time together helping out friends by jointly caring for their children, we're still just friends."

"And the picture of us kissing?" he demanded gruffly. "What do we say about that?"

Allison hesitated. Finally, throwing up her hands, she said, "We'll just both say that it didn't mean anything. It was just a brief kiss goodbye. A peck on the cheek that missed its target when things got awkward." Starting to feel embarrassed, she swallowed. "I mean, that could happen, couldn't it? Pictures can sometimes be deceptive."

He gave her a slow, critical once-over. "What about the *lovers* part?"

Heat moved from her chest into her neck, then her face. With effort, she inhaled sharply and kept her eyes locked with his. "Well, obviously, we wouldn't tell them that."

His tone hardened. "We'd lie."

"Maintain our privacy," she corrected.

"Lie," he argued.

Planting her hands on her hips, she glared up at him. He wasn't playing fair here. She'd been nothing but supportive when he'd had his shot at the big time... "Why are you being like this?"

Anger flared in his eyes. "For starters," he countered in a take-no-prisoners voice that set her pulse to racing, "I don't want to pretend I don't want to be with you when I do."

The ache in her throat grew exponentially. "I don't want that, either." Without warning, she found herself fighting back tears as the emotional ties they had forged this last week began to splinter.

He shrugged. "Then it should be simple."

Except it wasn't. Especially since, up to now, he had been so supportive of her work. Aware this could easily blow up into something neither of them wanted, she tried again. "Cade, you had your shot at the big time. You lived your dream. I haven't had mine, and I'm not going to lie to you," she said softly. "I want it."

Just as she wanted Cade to love her so much he would do anything to find a way for them to be together.

But he hadn't in the past, and he didn't now. So...

Cade scowled and shook his head in silent remonstration. "Yeah, I can see that," he said.

Allison struggled to hold on to what reason she

had left. Hands spread wide, she pointed out, "We *can* be together… We just can't act like it in public."

"Like I said." Hurt and resentment scored his low tone. "I don't want to lie. Adhering to half-truths… promising everyone I was one hundred percent ready to pitch…when I knew damn well I wasn't there yet…is what cost me my pro career, remember?"

"This is different! It isn't about your fitness as an athlete!"

"Doesn't matter. Adhering to any half-truth would definitely set a bad example and cost me the position as high school coach."

"And you're not willing to give that up," Allison said sadly, doing her best to contain her hurt.

"No."

Anger sparked. "So once again it's what you want that matters most."

Silence fell. His nostrils flared. "This is about *us*," he corrected. "But you're right about one thing. There is no way I am trading my soul for fame and fortune. For you or for me. Not ever again. And if you're smart, you won't do so, either."

"It doesn't have to be that cut-and-dried, Cade."

"Doesn't it?"

Clearly, he thought there was only one right way to proceed and one wrong.

"Listen to me, Cade," she pleaded softly, urging him to be reasonable. This was a terrible situation. But like the flooded upstairs carpet at the Bailey home, it could still be repaired. "With a little time, and the help of a good crisis manager, we can figure out a way to allow me to hold on to everything I've built thus far, as a successful single woman, and still let it be known I have a right to love *and* a private life."

Cold recognition lit his eyes when he realized they were talking about her brand again. "By just letting people make whatever assumptions they want to make."

"Yes!"

His dark brow lifted. "Like they did about me, during my big-time-bachelor days?"

Allison fell silent at the reproof in his gaze. There was no question the resulting gossip had really damaged his overall reputation. When she had believed it, it had made her think less of him, too.

"That kind of speculation would hurt both of us. And it would make me a poor role model to kids."

She couldn't argue his point. While having a sexy lover could ultimately help her, with her fans, it would harm him. As a prospective teacher and coach, he needed to consider that.

Her phone dinged. The message said the HITN executives were now about twenty minutes away. Panic rose. Especially when she saw all this back-and-forth hadn't budged him in the least.

"So what are you saying?" she asked penitently,

as her pulse began to race. "You won't help me buy time to try to work this out?"

He shook his head, implacable. "Not if it means shading the truth in any way."

"Which means what, then, exactly?" she asked helplessly, spreading her hands wide. She stared at him, aghast, as the realization of where this was heading finally set in. "We should just stop seeing each other?"

His jaw set. "Given the way you feel?" he returned roughly, as emotionally distant as he had ever been. "The values that you have? Doesn't seem to me that we have any other choice." He turned on his heel and left her to show herself out.

Chapter Sixteen

Two days later, Allison's doorbell rang. Hoping it might be Cade, having come to his senses, she rushed to answer it. Sarabeth stood on her porch, a stunning fruit basket and handcrafted white fudge in hand. "Hey, stranger," she said, glowing like a newlywed.

"Hey back." With a smile, Allison ushered her in. The two of them hadn't had a chance to really talk since she'd returned from Switzerland. "You are looking fabulous."

"I feel better than I have in years!"

Allison led her toward her kitchen, where she had coffee brewing. "How's Shawn?"

"He had an appointment with an orthopedic surgeon here yesterday, just to make sure all the healing is on track, and it is. His sister came in from Michigan to spend a little time with him. Which is how I'm able to run off and do a little Christmas shopping on my own, but I wanted to drop these off first." She set the gifts on the counter. "How are you doing? You look a little…" Sarabeth came even closer. "Have you been crying?"

All night, the past two nights, Allison thought. Figuring she might as well unburden herself to someone, she pushed past the tightness in her throat and told Sarabeth everything that had happened while they'd been gone.

Sarabeth slipped onto a stool. "And you haven't heard from Cade since you quarreled?"

"No," Allison admitted sadly.

"Well…" Her friend paused, searching for the upside. "At least he didn't disagree with you when you told *Personalities!* magazine that the story was incorrect, that the two of you weren't an item."

Allison brought out two mugs. "I didn't do that. I don't have those kinds of connections to get the magazine to issue a correction on the daily blog." Which was read by many more people than the actual magazine, as it happened, since the website was free.

"I heard Jennifer Moore of *City Lights* did get the new HITN TV show."

Allison nodded. Although she wasn't as heartbroken about that as she had expected to be. Maybe because she had come to realize that one of the best things about being an internet blogger was the ability to select her own topics and work at her own speed. She had not enjoyed constantly being expected to meet the network's often unreasonable demands. Nor had she appreciated the HITN execs' insistence on controlling the boundaries of her private life, and keeping it within her brand, when they had come to confront her about the gossip about her and Cade. So she had done what she had known in her heart was right, preserving her own freedom and integrity and taking herself out of the competition for the slot. Of course, by then it had been too late to admit how wrong she had been and patch things up with Cade. Having seen how angry and disillusioned he had been with her, she had known he would never forgive her. And the worst part was, knowing how self-centeredly she had behaved, she could hardly blame him.

Sarabeth stirred cream into her coffee. "What do you think this will mean for your career?"

Allison sipped. "Hard to say. I've had an awful lot of traffic on *My Cottage Life* the last few days. So, ultimately, maybe I will get more readers and, from that, more product advertising."

"Well, that's something."

But not what she had thought she wanted. Not even close, to be perfectly honest. Suppressing a sigh of disappointment, Allison forced herself to smile, prompting, "Tell me about you and Shawn."

Sarabeth brightened. "We've turned things around."

Allison had guessed as much, but it was nice to hear her say so. "I'm glad."

Sarabeth sobered, admitting, "We almost didn't, though."

Feeling there was a reason her friend wanted to talk about this now, Allison studied her. "Why not?"

Sarabeth sighed her regret. "We weren't being honest with ourselves, and each other, about what we were thinking and feeling. Instead, we let ourselves stay locked into erroneous expectations."

The pain of heartbreak surged. "Like what?"

Sarabeth's expression turned rueful. "Shawn thought I wanted him to bring in the maximum amount of income to be happy. And that he could balance out his long absences with moving us back here to my hometown."

Allison studied her friend. "Whereas you…?"

"Just missed him. And worried about all the time he was away from the quadruplets that he wouldn't be able to get back." Her shoulders slumped at the memory. "The thing is, I was starting to really resent him. And he felt it, and we know now, from some things the kids have started to tell us, that the kids were feeling the stress, too."

"So what's the plan?"

"Shawn's switching to a work-at-home job with

his company. It will mean less income, but he won't have to travel the way he has been. And that's what is really important to us. From now on, we're putting our marriage and family first." She paused. "Maybe you and Cade could work out something, too."

Allison's heart ached. "But what if it's too late? If you've done the unforgivable as far as the love of your life is concerned? And you've already blown your chance to be together? Not just once. But twice?"

Sarabeth looked her in the eye. "Take it from me and Shawn. If you're headed in the wrong direction, it's never too late to do a U-turn."

"You know, when we told you we wanted to throw a party to celebrate your new job, we did not expect you to spend the entire time out in the backyard, chopping wood for us," Carol Lockhart said.

Cade turned to his mom. He knew he had given her reason to worry about him in the past with some of the decisions he had made. He was sorry about that. "I'm fine, Mom." Brokenhearted. Disappointed and disillusioned. But otherwise okay.

Carol turned up the collar of her coat against the brisk winter wind. Her brow lifted. "Are you?"

Cade shrugged and went back to chopping wood. *Thwack, thwack, thwack.* "Just not in the best mood."

His mother moved to better see his face. "Because of Allison."

Cade scowled. "Why do you think she has anything to do with it?" They were over. Plain and simple.

"Honey, everyone in the county heard about the fact you were spending time together again. We were all hoping it was going to be a permanent arrangement this time."

Cade picked up the splintered pieces and put them on the growing pile beside the stump. "*Arrangement* is the right word all right," he said bitterly.

Carol's glance narrowed. "What are you talking about?"

Grimly, he admitted, "I didn't realize it at the time I started getting involved with her again, but the only way Allison was going to be with me was if I didn't interfere with her brand." And that still stung. More than he wanted to admit.

His mother's expression lit up. "Ah, yes. *My Cottage Life.*"

"Yeah, well, that cottage of hers doesn't come with a man."

His mother chuckled. "So, spend time at your place. I'm pretty sure she'd be welcome there."

"Mom…"

"I'm serious." Carol moved to block his way when he started to get more wood. She planted both hands on her hips. "I know you've always been a proud person. Stubborn, too! From the first moment you came to live with us as a foster kid. But I thought you had gotten past all that," she worried out loud.

Cade frowned. "I have!"

"Then why are you letting whatever this is stop you from pursuing her, when it's clear to me, anyway, and the way you're whacking the heck out of that wood, that all you *really* want is to pursue her!"

Bitterness tightened his gut. It was true. These days, he had no problem asking for what he wanted and needed. With anyone but Allison, that was.

Aware his mom was still awaiting an explanation, he said, "Because I can't go back to—" *wanting what I can't have and* "—a life that is nothing but a facade."

"The way it was during your pro career," his mom guessed.

Cade nodded. "Always running around with one or even two women on my arm. Pretending that I had it all, when all I really wanted was…" He choked up.

"Allison."

Emotion clogged his throat. Curtly, he nodded. "I'm never going to feel about anyone else the way I feel about her." He had always known it. Even when he hadn't wanted to admit it.

"Then go find her," his mother retorted in exasperation. "And tell her that."

He raked a hand through his hair. "How can I? From what I heard and read in the news, I'm the reason she damaged her brand and lost that TV gig she wanted. I'm sure she wants nothing to do with me. Now or ever again." Not that he would ever allow either of them to be put in a position where they had to lie. Or even spout half-truths.

His mom nodded. "That could be true. She might never forgive you."

He looked up, stunned to hear the possibility put so bluntly. Especially by his mom, who was the biggest champion of love and commitment he knew.

"Or...like you," Carol pushed empathetically, "Allison could be sadder and more brokenhearted than she ever thought she could be. But too stubborn and scared to find out if you're feeling the same way."

His mom waited for her words to sink in, then hugged him close and finished sagely, "You spent your whole life chasing dreams, Cade Lockhart. Don't let this quest be the one that finally eludes you."

Allison stood on the front porch of her cottage, staring at her front door, trying to figure out if she had forgotten anything. *Before* she made the fateful call...

"Gorgeous..." a low voice behind her said.

Heart leaping into her throat, Allison spun around. Cade stood there. Like her, surprisingly dressed up for a dateless Monday evening.

Unless he wasn't dateless.

Because, freshly showered and shaven, in a tweed charcoal sport coat, light blue button-up and tie, dark-rinse jeans and boots, he certainly looked like he was ready to chase after someone.

"Are you talking about the wreath on my front door?" she quipped lightly, so very happy to see him, no matter why he was here.

She had missed him desperately!

He tilted his head, letting his gaze drift over her, taking in her formfitting red knit dress and heels. "Hmm... I think I like the lady standing in front of it better," he murmured in that rough-tender voice she loved so much.

Tears threatened. She knew she couldn't afford to get this wrong, again. "It's starting to get really cold," she said inanely.

He mounted the steps. Standing next to her, he swooped an arm about her waist. Looking both hopeful and wary, he bent down to whisper in her ear. "Maybe we should find a place that's warm, then."

"Good idea." She leaned into the curve of his body, savoring his solid male strength. Turning to him, her heart pounding like a wild thing in her chest, she inhaled his cedarwood musk. They could work this out, she told herself boldly. All they had to do was try.

She smiled, ignoring the growing knot of emotion in her throat. "Why don't you come inside?"

His expression serious and intent, he took her hand. "Love to."

Aware her knees were shaking, she escorted him

through the door. His gaze widened as he took in the intimate setting. A fire roared in the grate. Soft holiday music played. A table was beautifully set— for two. A bottle of champagne chilled in a bucket of ice. "Looks like I might have interrupted something," he said, his expression unreadable.

She held on to his hand. The steady warmth of his touch imbued her with courage. "Actually," she retorted, looking him in the eye, "you were exactly the man I was hoping to see this evening."

His lips curved into a slow, sexy grin.

She knew they could make love right now, and it would be wonderful, but she wanted more than just the physical this time. And that meant they were going to have to be honest and direct with each other and talk their problems through.

"Congratulations on your new job," she said.

"Thank you." He paused to squeeze her hand. "I'm sorry you didn't get yours."

Despite everything that had gone on, she could see his regret was sincere. "I appreciate that," she said, surprised to see how little the opportunity meant to her now, "but it was probably for the best."

Her sober admission had him narrowing his eyes. "Why do you say that?"

Her voice dropped a confiding notch. "Because the brand they wanted to promote isn't who I am anymore."

For a moment, he was skeptical, and she could

certainly understand why. Finally, he said, "Sure about that?"

She led him to the sofa and sat down beside him. "I've been doing a lot of thinking the past few weeks," she admitted self-effacingly. "The single life is great when being on your own is all you want."

Understanding lit his eyes. And she realized that he really did understand, that what was important to her was important to him, too. "I get that," he said softly.

She squeezed his fingers, continuing affably, "But when you find the person you want to spend the rest of your life with…again…it loses its luster."

His espresso eyes twinkled. "Do tell," he said, pulling her to her feet and gazing at her as if he couldn't wait to hear more.

Allison admired the handsome planes of his face, the masculine slant of his lips. "Oh, Cade, I'm so sorry." She encircled her arms about his neck and stepped even closer. "I should never have asked you to lie so I could get a job." She kept her eyes locked with his and stipulated carefully, "Because it was never going to be worth it. Selling your soul never is."

He brought her all the way into his arms and ran a hand gently down her spine. "And I should have never pretended that I could walk away," he admitted with the same soul-baring honesty. His gaze drifted lovingly over her face before returning to her eyes. "Because the truth is, you…we…are worth fighting for. And I didn't fight for us the way I should have. Not years ago, when I let *my* ambition tear us apart," he admitted with heartfelt regret. "And I certainly didn't do so the other day."

She snuggled against his tall, strong body. Tenderness wafted through her, fueling an even deeper reverence and need. "But you're ready to do so now."

"With every fiber of my being." He cupped her face in his hands and kissed her sweetly. "I love you, Allison Meadows. I always have. Always will."

The tears she'd been holding back finally spilled over her lashes. "I love you, too, Cade."

"Then what do you say we make it official." Eyes dark with emotion, he withdrew a ring box from his pocket and dropped down on one knee. "Allison Meadows, will you marry me?"

And just like that, everything she had ever wanted and dreamed of was hers for the taking. "*Yes*, Cade Lockhart!" She dropped down to her knees, too, and kissed him again, even more joyously this time. "I absolutely will…"

Epilogue

December 24th, one year later...

"Okay, Miss Allison and Mr. Cade, you can come in now!" the quadruplets said in unison.

Grinning, Allison and Cade clasped hands and crossed the portal into her cottage. At first glance, the cozy abode looked just as it had when they stepped outside to await the dispensing of the girls' holiday magic.

"Notice anything different?" Amber asked while petting the black Lab, who had come over to "help," too.

"Zeus's collar?" Cade guessed. It was a red-and-green plaid with jingle-bell tags on it instead of the usual red leather.

"No, silly," Sienna said. "He was wearing that when we got here!"

Cade's expression turned rueful. "It's very pretty, as are all of you."

All four were wearing identical green dresses with black tights and shoes.

"Thank you, but you still have to notice what we did!" Jade, who took all things crafty very seriously, said.

Hazel did a cartwheel across the living area, landing next to the foyer table. She angled her head in the direction she wanted them to look.

Allison clapped her hands in surprise. "Oh, gosh, it's a new poinsettia!"

"And it's specially fancy because it's got red flowers. And white!" Jade pointed out.

"I love it." Allison grinned.

"Me, too," Cade said.

"Keep looking," Amber advised, while their parents looked on approvingly.

Cade found the Santa plate, bearing homemade sugar cookies with an abundance of colored icing and sprinkles. "Oh, wow," he said. "These look delicious!"

Sienna jumped up and down. "Have some!"

Cade took one and handed half to Allison. "Delicious," she decreed.

"Really good," Cade concurred.

"Notice anything else?" Amber asked excitedly, wordlessly encouraging them to look up. Allison and Cade did. Sure enough, right above the cookies was a sprig.

"Mistletoe!" Allison and Cade said in unison, then burst into merry laughter.

"It's what caused you to get married, and Daddy and Mommy to be so happy, too," Jade declared.

Hazel threw up her arms in joy. "Kiss! Kiss! Kiss!" she shouted. Her sisters joined in.

Cade wrapped an arm about Allison's waist and brought her close, thinking she had never looked lovelier or more glowing with good health than she did at that moment. "Don't mind if I do," he murmured, bending his head to brush his lips across the softness of hers.

She melted against him happily.

So happily that who knew what would have happened had they not had an audience. Saving the rest for later, he drew back.

"And now for the last gift." Jade pointed to the festively wrapped package on the sofa.

"Go on," Sarabeth urged, her eyes shining.

"Open it," Shawn said.

Cade took Allison by the hand and led her over to sit down. He let her do the honors as the girls and Zeus crowded around. They bounced up and down elatedly while she removed the ribbon and outer paper. Her hands trembling slightly, Allison opened up the box and parted the tissue paper, gasping in delight at the pink and blue onesies.

"It's for your new babies!" the girls shouted happily.

Her eyes filling, Allison beamed. "Thank you!"

"Group hug!" Cade said, holding out his arms.

"Okay, girls," Shawn interjected when they'd all finished embracing. "We have more presents to deliver today."

"Bye! Merry Christmas! To your twin babies, too!" They took Zeus's leash and headed out the door.

Very much alone, Allison settled back on the sofa before the fire.

"Hard to believe how much has happened in just a year, isn't it?" she murmured.

Cade brought over two cups of mulled cider. "It is." He snuggled beside her.

Allison had rejected the offer of a show from another cable network and started her own YouTube channel instead. Her blog had started focusing on the effect unexpected change had on a person's life. And would soon incorporate motherhood, too. Meanwhile, Cade was knocking it out of the park as the new high school coach and would soon be prepping for his second season with his team.

Through it all, they had been there for each other. First, as an engaged couple, and then as husband and wife, and now they were expecting twins. A boy and a girl, the sonogram had shown.

"I was thinking," Allison murmured, sliding over

onto his lap, "now that your bachelor abode has sold, maybe the cottage should become my place of business instead of our home."

It was a little cramped, Cade acknowledged, but he hadn't minded because he knew how much it meant to her. "You'd be okay with that?" he asked. Because they could add on, although doing so would further reduce the minuscule backyard.

Allison nodded. "I think it's time I let go of the past, and that we should find a place for our future. Together…"

"One with a lot more kid space?"

"And room for a family pet?" Her cheeks turned a becoming pink. "I know that you've been wanting a dog, and I do, too."

"Well, now that you mention it," Cade drawled, shifting her off his lap and rising.

Right on cue, a car parked in front of the house.

"I've got something for you, too." He opened the door as his sister MacKenzie came up the walk, wicker basket in hand.

"What in the…?" Allison gasped as a fluffy white Maltese puppy peeked her head over the top of the basket. "Oh…" Tears of joy flowed from her eyes. "Cade!"

"I thought this might make you happy," he said gruffly, lifting the puppy out of the basket and handing her over to Allison.

"You're right!" She cuddled the pup close, and then kissed Cade blissfully.

MacKenzie laughed, teasing, "I'd tell you to get a room, but you've got a whole cottage…!"

"Thank you, too," Allison told MacKenzie.

"Hey!" The other woman's eyes shimmered as she leaned in for a hug. "You've made my brother so happy. There's nothing I wouldn't do. For either of you."

"Want to come in?" Cade asked.

"Nope." MacKenzie turned on her heel and bounded back down the walk. She grinned at them over her shoulder. "I'm headed back to Fort Worth! I've got my own secret plans to attend to!"

"Think she'll ever get married?" Allison asked, as MacKenzie drove away.

"Not unless she ever figures out that Griffith Montgomery is the only guy for her."

"Hmm."

Noting how cute his wife looked with the puppy snuggled in her arms, Cade pulled her close. "But let's not worry about them when we have so very much to rejoice in."

"Agreed." Allison kissed him sweetly and tenderly. "Merry Christmas," she whispered.

He returned her kiss and gazed down at her adoringly. "Merry Christmas to you, too, my love." Together, they headed back inside to celebrate the holiday with their new puppy.

* * * * *

*Watch for more books in Cathy Gillen Thacker's
Lockharts Lost & Found miniseries!
Book #3 coming May 2021,
only from Harlequin Special Edition!*

WE HOPE YOU ENJOYED
THIS BOOK FROM

HARLEQUIN
SPECIAL
EDITION

Believe in love. Overcome obstacles. Find happiness.

Relate to finding comfort and strength in the
support of loved ones and enjoy the journey
no matter what life throws your way.

6 NEW BOOKS AVAILABLE EVERY MONTH!

HSEHALO2020

COMING NEXT MONTH FROM

HARLEQUIN
SPECIAL EDITION

Available October 27, 2020

#2797 HIS CHRISTMAS CINDERELLA
Montana Mavericks: What Happened to Beatrix?
by Christy Jeffries
Jordan Taylor has it all—except someone to share his life with. What he really wants for Christmas is to win the heart of Camilla Sanchez, the waitress he met at a charity ball. Camilla thinks they are too different to make it work, but Jordan is determined to prove her wrong—in three weeks!

#2798 SOMETHING ABOUT THE SEASON
Return to the Double C • by Allison Leigh
When wealthy investor Gage Stanton arrives at Rory McAdams's struggling guest ranch, she's suspicious. Is he just there to learn the ranching ropes or to get her to give up the property? But their holiday fling soon begins to feel like anything but—until Gage's shocking secret threatens to derail it.

#2799 THE LONG-AWAITED CHRISTMAS WISH
Dawson Family Ranch • by Melissa Senate
Maisey Clark, a struggling single mom, isn't going to suddenly start believing in Christmas magic. So what if Rex Dawson found her childhood letter to Santa and wants to give her and her daughter the best holiday ever? He's just passing through, and love is for suckers. If only his kisses didn't feel like the miracle she always hoped for...

#2800 MEET ME UNDER THE MISTLETOE
Match Made in Haven • by Brenda Harlen
Haylee Gilmore *always* made practical decisions—except for one unforgettable night with Trevor Blake! Now she's expecting his baby, and the corporate cowboy wants to do the right thing. But the long-distance mom-to-be refuses to marry for duty—she wants his heart.

#2801 A SHERIFF'S STAR
Home to Oak Hollow • by Makenna Lee
Oak Hollow, Texas, was supposed to be a temporary stop between Tess's old life in Boston and the new one in Houston. But when her daughter, Hannah, wraps handsome police chief Anson Curry—who also happens to be their landlord—around her little finger, Tess is tempted for the first time in a long time.

#2802 THEIR CHRISTMAS BABY CONTRACT
Blackberry Bay • by Shannon Stacey
With IVF completely out of her financial reach, Reyna Bishop is running out of time to have the child she so very much wants. Her deal with Brady Nash is purely practical: no emotion, no expectation, no ever-after. It's foolproof...till the time she spends with Brady and his warm, loving family leaves Reyna wanting more than a baby...

HSECNM1020

"Sweet dreams, little one," he said and stepped out of
the room.

She took off Hannah's shoes and jeans, then tucked
her in for the night. With a bolstering breath, she braced
herself for being alone with her fantasy man.

He stood in the center of the living room, looking
around like he'd never seen his own house. She
followed Anson's gaze to the built-in shelves she'd
filled with precious and painful memories. Things she
wasn't ready to share with him. Before he could ask any
questions, she opened the front door.

"Even though we were coerced, thank you for carrying her home. And for the house tour." Their "moment" in his bedroom flashed before her. *Damn, why'd I bring that up?*

"Anytime." Anson's blue-eyed gaze danced with amusement before he ducked his head and stepped outside. "Sleep well, Tess."

Fat chance of that.

She closed the door to prevent herself from watching him walk away. Tonight, Anson hadn't treated her indifferently like before and, in fact, seemed to be fighting his own temptations. Sometimes shutters would fall over his eyes as he distanced himself, then she'd blink and he'd wear his devil's grin, drawing her in with flirtation. Maybe he wasn't as immune to their attraction as she'd thought.

"I can't figure you out, Chief Anson Curry. But why am I even bothering?"

Don't miss
A Sheriff's Star by Makenna Lee,
available November 2020 wherever
Harlequin Special Edition books and ebooks are sold.

Harlequin.com

HSEEXP1020